T.W.CLAWSON

Volume 3

Printed in the United States of America

First Printing, 2023

ISBN Ebook - 978-1-7364618-7-7
Paperback - 978-1-7364618-6-0

The Odd Empire
675 NW 2nd Ave
Canby, OR, 97013

www.TWClawson.com

Front cover art by:
Aubrey C. Sanders
@aubreyc.sanders

Penny Lich Logo designed by:
Barbara Guttman
www.marteani.art

These three stories are dedicated to:

Alexa Tibbles
Britt Winchester
Cam Clawson
Gage Runkle
JT Owens

Thank you for playing with me.
What color was the water?

You came Back! I must be funny!

T.W. CLAWSON

A Game of HOMES

"Welcome back everyone!" Moses says to the early morning crew of the Penny Lich. He stands by the fireplace holding his mug of coffee, addressing the white sun-filled room. His warmth and that of the hearth battle against the frigid cold of the Gaze month air. Even more frigid looks come from the waking guild members.

"The Gaze month is upon us," Moses continues. "So, you know, more visitors to the Penny Lich looking for warmth and relaxation, good songs from the new bards coming to town, and great drinks provided by our very own Gwen Ling. Means we'll have an opportunity to strike up more conversation, which means? Anyone? Anyone? New quests for our little band of adventurers. So remember to enjoy the newcomers, but be aware that we're on the clock, and we're trying to sell our services."

"You got us up this early so you could tell us that?" Aarik sips on coffee and lounges in his wooden chair. "That could have been a scroll on the quest board."

"Actually that was just my opener. We actually have a special guest coming toda--"

"It's not an opener if it's not a joke." Brohn raises his hand but doesn't wait to be called on.

"It opened the meeting...." Moses responds. "Like I was saying, we need to be on our best behav--"

"But by definition, an opener is a joke that opens the meeting. A funny story or anecdote," Brohn continues.

"He's right," Elliot says, sitting at the table closest to Moses.

"It doesn't matter, I was just opening with that, can I please get to the next bit? We have a cleric from Thickstem and her daughter coming to stay with us."

"I'm just saying, for a paladin, you're not that good at orating."

"Hey!" Moses points at Brohn. "I was number one in my orating class. I'm so good with my oral abilities I was given a badge of honor!"

The guild snickers.

"No, no, no!" Moses shouts, "Don't make this a gross thing."

"Hey, guys," Elliot says from his table, "give the man a break, he just wants to prove to you how good he is with his mouth."

Chuckles.

Aarik puts his mug down, "Everyone calm down, Moses just wants to use his mouth and help us get a head."

Chuckles.

Moses throws up his hands. "Please, this is not appropriate and we have people coming."

The room erupts in laughter.

"He is so good at oral he makes people come on command," Sycilia laughs. The room continues to laugh with her.

"Fine," Moses says. "Fine, you guys wanna spend our first meeting back being gross, then go ahead. I'm sure however good I was at orating, Aarik has had more experience than anyone. He knows how to get a head faster than a royal ass kisser." Moses points to Aarik; the guild laughs at him. "And Brohn knows a thing or two about fisting his opponents, am I right?"

The tavern erupts as Brohn holds up his fists in mock anger.

"And don't get me started with Elliot...." Moses says, the guild waits for the drop, "They say anything could happen to a young cleric in the dark and mysterious dungeons of the Candle Crypts. Why you might ask? Simple, it's full of clerics!"

"Excuse me!?"

The guild turns around to see Mio, the cleric of Aster, and her daughter, Mila, standing at the door. Moses' eyes are wide in fear and embarrassment; the rest of the room slinks down as though they had been caught by a parent. Ella shouts over the bar, "Don't worry, Mio, That was just his opener, there's still more to come."

Several moments pass as Moses apologizes and takes Mio and her daughter into Elliot's office, while Elliot takes over the morning meeting.

"Do we have to start over with a new opener?" Gwen asks.

"No, I'm gonna get straight to the point," Elliot says. "So as you can see, we have a guest staying with us. So we'll need to be as accommodating as possible."

"I can accommodate her," Aarik says as he watches the door to Elliot's office close.

Snap snap!

Aarik turns and Sycilia pulls his attention with her snapping. "Down boy, she's a cleric. She's not gonna sleep with you."

"I mean, she could." Ella says, "if that's who you wanna sleep with." Aarik glances at Ella and winks.

"No, just taking notice. Like a fine painting."

"Aarik," Elliot says, "can I continue?"

"Yes, dad." Aarik says, sipping his coffee again.

"Moses and I are going to be hosting a small group

of youngsters, including Mila, for a local Magecore fair. Hadvar is working on lunch for them, and Brohn, we'll probably need your help carousing the youngsters. While we do that, you three–" Elliot points to Sycilia, Ella and Aarik, "will be moving your stuff out of my rooms."

"What?" Sycilia chokes on her eggs.

"You three are taking up the only three available rooms we have. Cleric Mio and Mila need a room to stay in, and it's come to my attention that everyone thinks they can live here rent free."

"Yeah, cause we've been living here rent free...." Aarik says.

"It's not my fault you got thrown out for practicing magic in the attic," Elliot says.

"No, it's her fault." Aarik points to Ella.

"Don't blame her." Sycilia slaps Aarik. "She only comes over to teach you magic cause you invite her."

"What can I say? A hot redhead that stays up late and makes magic with me? I'm addicted."

"I don't make magic, Aarik," Ella retorts. "I do magic. And really, doing magic is incorrect. I channel magic and perform magic. If I do anything, it's rituals. I do the rituals. Though, now that I think about it, I would be performing those as well. Performing rituals, incantations."

"I think performing magic implies a trick, like a bard's show," Gwen says.

"So in this case doing magic would be the right term?" Ella asks.

"Fine," Aarik says. "I'm sorry a hot redhead likes to come do magic to me."

The guild groans.

"I'm on fire today."

"I'm gonna light you on fire if you don't shut up,"

Sycilia threatens.

"Was that an intimidation check?" Aarik rolls his eyes. He straightens up when he sees that both Sycilia and Elliot are staring him down, "Ok, fine, success."

"You can't just kick us out, Elliot." Sycilia says after scaring Aarik.

"Sycilia," Elliot says with a softer tone, "I'm not just kicking you out. I spoke to the Mistress, and she says there is a court session today. You can go there and bring your case to the royal houses and earn a place."

"So we have to pack, move all our stuff, and do these royal nerds a favor, just so we can have somewhere to sleep tonight?" Aarik asks.

"Yes."

"That seems like a lot to do in one day."

"Hence why we got you up so early."

The Valeward Ravine is where the royal manor and houses of aristocracy have been carved into the earth. The small gorge funnels into a collection of summits that offer a natural wall. The facing walls of the rocky landscape curves out to a wide field that looks over the city from its high place in the western hills. The lower stories with arching architecture lead into the guild halls, the upper floors balconies for the upper echelon to look out on the capital field.

As the ravine moves back to the peaks, the trees take more shape, pampered and trimmed to perfection. Several arches stand over the road in the middle of the gully. They act as flagpoles, with each family represented by a banner hanging from their crest tree. All families represented, all guilds present, all people important gathered in the field of the courtyard.

Looming from the very back of the ravine is a massive ten story building, etched into the rocks of the mountain.

"The trees don't die?" Sycilia asks.

"Magic," Aarik answers.

"That's your answer to everything."

"Sometimes it's right."

"Is that why it's warm up here, too?" Sycilia pulls her coat off. The chill air of the month of Gaze gives way to something more comfortable. She folds the leather jacket up and wraps it around her bag, then looks up at Aarik. He seems to be investigating the area.

"If I had to guess, I'd say it's the heat from the volcano over there."

"Volcano!?"

"Yeah," Aarik says with a smirk. "Don't you remember going to Thickstem village? That was a volcano."

"Yeah, but that was a couple days away!" Sycilia becomes suddenly aware of the ground. The warmth, the fragility. Magma laying in wait below. The ground could crack open at any time and let loose a flow of lava to consume her. Her eyes dart back and forth in fear. Aarik realizes she's going to freak out.

"You're about to freak out, aren't you?" Aarik asks.

"No," Sycilia says quickly. She is indeed about to freak out when Aarik points to the peak on the left.

"You see that billowing smoke?"

"Yeah."

"Maybe volcano is the wrong term, this is more a dormant... hot hill. That's the vent. As long as that smoke is white, we're fine. The moisture from the upper part of the mountain is steaming and releasing from there. Now if it goes black, then we have a problem."

"Why?"

"Cause it means that the rock below is burning as magma climbs in elevation. The rocks would be releasing oxidized minerals, and they are smoking as they come out. So we'll know if something bad is about to happen. Does that help?"

Sycilia focuses on the white plume of smoke and breathes a little easier. She nods as the anxiety begins to subside. "Yeah, actually. That really helps." She laughs and punches Aarik on the arm. "When did you become a volcano expert?"

"Volcanologist. And I went to the premiere academy in Yonder Valley. That's what all mom's money went towards."

"Is that where it all went? Crazy. I was never informed that your education cost a thing," she says in a mock tone. The undertone of something strings along in her voice. Aarik catches it.

"I mean, I would have been happy to trade places with you, the favorite daughter of Valley Gate."

"Favorite daughter?" playful tones give way to buried truth. Sycilia can feel things uncover from her past. Things meant to stay dead begin to break out from their graves. She clicks her tongue and points her finger. "You know how much I had to do to make my name?"

"Send out an invitation?" Aarik smirks, continuing to walk ahead. "I imagine it on parchment wrapped in lambs skin to sh--"

"You think you're better than me?!" Sycilia puts her hand on his shoulder. Anger rises and makes it hard to keep her hand off the hilt of her sword.

"Whoa!" Aarik says, throwing his hands up. "I was just joking around." He looks at the hand itching for her hilt. His gaze shifts and the smirk stays, but his eyes become concerned. "That's what brothers and sisters do, they joke around. Remember?"

Suddenly Sycilia catches herself. She was preparing to attack her brother. Her flesh and blood. Terror replaces anger and she relents. Her body begins quivering in fear.

"My Divine," she says. "I'm so sorry, Aarik. That was–that was uncalled for."

"You ok?"

"No, I mean, yeah. Yeah, I'm ok. I just–Conclave–I'm so sorry. I spent so long on the streets, so long with the Rummagers. I just–I get a little overwhelmed by us joking around all the time, you know? Giving each other crap."

"Hey, I'm sorry." Aarik puts his hand on her hand. His strength pulses through into her body and comfort wells up inside. "I was out of line. I'm just excited to be with my sister again, doing all this crazy stuff, living life like an adventurer. I think I forget sometimes that we still have to get to know each other, you know?"

Sycilia sees her mother in Aariks eyes. The woman was hard and direct, but when she wanted to be, she was as kind and giving as the spring. Sycilia taps the hand holding her hand.

"Thanks, Aarik. I appreciate that."

"I know I'm not better than you, really and truly." Aarik says. They start walking toward the great Valeward Castle, and Aarik smiles as he says, "I'm just smarter than you."

The throne of Valeward is as empty as it has been for 200 years. The king, being a bit busy with being dead and all kinda keeps them a bit preoccupied to join in the royal court precessions. Most of the royal houses are fins with this, as it means to there's no one to think themselves over important. That sentiment is tolerated on by the royal houses themselves.

The king's table, sit on an risen stage, empty and waiting for a return to true order. Gold rimming the edge of marble and pearlescent stone. The feet of the table are carved like trunks of trees, its canopy the resting place for parchment and food. This great and beautiful furniture is alone–, and unused.

The rest of the room is filled with ornate and overly impressive tables for each house represented. None dare to overtake the dead kings table, as no royal blooded Valewardian dares to take the throne. Who would want to usurp the kingdom of a dragon. That would piss a dragon off, real bad. Ain't nobody gonna put that evil on themselves.

"Do we just go sit there?" Aarik nudges Sycilia, pointing at the king's table. Her lips tighten as he makes his joke.

"Oh, come on. I was joking."

"No you weren't. You think you're smarter than me, and I hate you for it."

"You don't hate me."

"Oh, I think I do," Sycilia says as she enters the mingling crowd of royalty. "Besides you shouldn't have a problem finding a solution to our problem since you're so smart." She disappears into a crowd of people that gather between the tables and discuss politics, the future of the kingdom, and a menagerie of other boring topics.

"Well, if I am smarter than you, then I'll figure out where we can stay, then I'll show you." Aarik looks around. "As I say to myself in a public space." He spots a waiter making his way through the crowd handing out food and drink.

"Two of my favorite things on a platter. Looks like I have a heading," Aarik disappears into the crowd.

Sycilia bows to Count Frellman. A regal and fit man in tight clothes and an outrageous hair-do looks her over.

"Who is this Aunty Hera?"

The Old woman leading Sycilia to a young count, speaks with excitement at the gossip Syscilia has brought her, "She's been kicked out by her forlorn lover, my dear. She works for a guild near the docks. It all sounds quite delicious. A real juicy story, my dear."

"Juicy?"

"Well, from the way you talk about him, it would seem like you two have a real connection, and you're besties with his ex? Quite scandalous."

"No, no, Countess Hera, it's not like that at all. I mean, yeah, he's great. Like, he listens, and he's really caring, and he's fierce, but not, like, overly macho," Sycilia says.

"A real catch.,"

"No, but I don't, I mean, we're not--"

"Oh." The woman says, holding a pair of tiny glasses in front of her crows feet ridden eyes. "I understand. And now you need space from this boy of yours."

"He's not my boy. I mean, he's not a boy. He's a man, and a perfectly grown and respectable man who needs to kick me out of his tavern to help make more business."

"My poor, dear. I understand."

"No, no I don't think you do." Sycilia laughs, annoyed.

"Either way, she is willing to do just about anything to earn a place to live"

"Anything, eh?" Frellman says with a smirk.

"Whoa, hold up, that sounds very weird." Sycilia throws her hands up. The man is good looking, as most count's are but he's not attractive enough to get away with anything he wants. No man is.

"I'm sorry, that was a bad joke," Frellman says. He bows with respect toward her and holds his hand out. Perfectly manicured, no evidence of a hard day's work. She takes the hand gently, contrasting his with a darker skinned, scar covered, calloused hand.

"My aunt has a bad habit of saying the wrong thing at the right time, and I have learned to make amusement of it."

"I'd say I make the right comment at the wrong time," Lady Hera says.

"Yeah, well, either way, I'm not here to beg or anything." Sycilia feels an uneasy joke growing around her. She knows that she is the butt of it, but can't place it. "A scorned lover, conflicted by his ex and her," Hera theater whispers to her nephew.

"Drop it Hera."

"There's no need to justify it," Frellmen's perfect hand cuts off the sentence welling up in her throat. "We Wies are a charitable family and are eager to work with our people. I do happen to have a loft on the docks. Quite nice, too; furnished with many amenities fit for a royal house. It was bought and built for my father and his–" he looks at his nails for a moment, then flicks his eyes back up at Sycilia, "Unsavory rendezvous."

Sycilia squirms a bit. "Ew."

"Yes, ew indeed, and to top it off, his murder was within the same walls, at the hands of a scorned lover."

"Oh my Divine." Sycilia coils back. She realizes that there is danger for everyone in this world, even those in luxury.

"Yes, well, that's what he gets for leading a double life. Or rather, a quadruple life. The man was a pig, and I'm certain that the kingdom will benefit from my sturdy and talented hands." Frellman raises his eyebrow toward Sycilia, a look of smug attraction; her heart beats in a terror she had buried long ago.

"My god, Deru," Hera says. "This is a woman in need of a home, as her lover has abandoned her, and you hit on her?"

"Again, I just need to make it clear that I have no lover. He's my boss, not my lover."

"Juicier and juicier," the woman says with a crinkled smile. This woman sees her as a plot device, and not a person. The less said, the shorter the story will be at her tea party later.

"I need to make it clear that my brother and I are looking for an apartment together. Is this death loft of yours suitable for us?"

"Brother and sister, eh?" Hera says.

"Settle down Hera," Sycilia says. "Separate rooms. Regular brother-sister relationship."

"Yes, of course. The apartment has two fully furnished bedrooms. By all means it's a pleasant little home for the underprivileged."

"Underprivileged?"

"The, uh, working class." The first break in his perfect facade. He turns to dismiss his aunt and grabs two drinks, offering one to Sycilia. The wine bubbles in the glass and Sycilia remembers the last party she went to with bubbly wine. The anger is replaced by guilt; her stomach turns and she refuses the drink.

"No thank you. I'm technically on the job. What

does this loft cost?"

"It's affordable, I assure you." Frellman drinks her drink and holds his. "But the fact remains that it is highly sought after. Getting in will be the hard part."

"Aren't you in charge of who gets in?"

"Yes."

"So it isn't that hard."

"Well," Frellman says with a faux pouting face. He extends the corners of his mouth down, and his lower lip outward. But his eyes delight in the problem. "That's just the thing, I'm going out of my way to get you this home, in an afternoon no doubt. What is it you can do for me?"

"What? You're extorting me?"

"My dear, this is how things work here. Power is exchanged, but not for nothing. Everyone here knows that they must give something to get something."

"You're getting my hard earned money."

"I can have anyone's hard earned money. Why would I want yours?"

"I–I don't--" The familiar tone of his voice gets to her. She shakes with anger from the condescension, the lofty ego. He is the same, he's exactly the same as Henderson. She was speaking to him again. And for a second she flashes back, the sword, the fingerbeast, attuning to the blade of the Sandren.

"Hello Rose Petal." The voice echos, she feels faint, her body begins to shut down. She scrunches her face and pulls herself back into the moment.

"No." She points her finger at Henderson–wait, it's Frellman. His face snaps back to the smug Wies man. "If you don't want my money, I'll go elsewhere." She turns to leave when his perfect hand grabs her shoulder.

She whips around with her hand on her hilt. He

cocks his eyebrow again. She can see the fear behind the composure. She's seen it before.

"So you and your family hang out here in the king's court all day, talking about this and that?" Aarik says as he drinks a glass of wine. The man he speaks to is bald, decorated, and has a faint glow of silver in his eyes.

"Well, we are one of the more prestigious families in the royal court," the man says, drinking wine in imitation. "We are included in the majority of the major goings ons of the kingdom."

"How..." Aarik gives the man a pass, down and up, "attractive."

The man smiles and a slight blush passes under his cheeks. Aarik smiles and remembers the rush of romance. The tingles that come along with acceptance and pleasure.

"How is it you got into the court today?" the man asks. "Our gatherings are usually closed to the public."

"We came on behalf of our boss. We work for the Penny Lich Guild."

"The what guild?"

"The Penny Lich," Aarik says.

"Which house does that belong to?" the man asks.

"I don't.... Uh, I don't understand."

"Each guild is controlled by a royal house." The man points to the tables around the room. "The Clowder Clan, my family, we control the Trades Guild. The Rovians control the Knights Guild, putting them pretty high up in favor with the council. The Gerells control the Study of Art, the Denier's have the temples, and then there's the Summerhills, the D'qoury family, Jalessioums, and the Wies."

"That's only eight."

"What?"

Aarik leans in, "That's only eight families, there's ten tables."

"Sure, well, obviously the king's table. But it's been empty since before the Turncoat Conflict. The Virgil Empire cut them out of the picture a long time ago."

"And table ten?" Aarik asks. The Clowder man turns and points to a table with a single person sitting at it. She has tight pulled back hair and a stiff collar.

"The Mistress?" Aarik asks.

"The Evergreen Family. They control the Magecore. Or rather, she...controls the Magecore." The man turns back around and asks again, "Who did you say you work for?"

"I think technically, I work for her."

"Again, I apologize," Count Frellman says.

His words are like honey. They drip from his mouth and soothe her mind. If she was smarter, she would have known a spell had been cast on her.

"You have to understand that my family, we are the royal house for the seat of Deru. The God of pain, of truth. We run the guild's responsible for torture, investigation, and spycraft. It is in my nature to push people."

"And It's in my nature to push back." Sycilia pulls her arm out from his grasp. It's tighter than she expected, but still nothing to her. She could crush his skull in five seconds. This helps her relax a bit. Being slightly attracted to his glowing eyes helps.

"I understand, and that's why I think you are the perfect candidate for my loft, if you would do one thing for me."

"What?"

"I want you to be the pug on my Scatterbattle duo."

"What?"

"I happen to be in need of a new duo for the games, and with your build and the fire I see behind your eyes, I think you would be perfect for a pug. If you think your brother would be willing to be your magician, you two could play for House Weis and earn the loft."

"That's it? You want me to play a game of Scatterbattle?"

"Well, this weekend's tournament. But that's only if you can convince your brother. And based on an educated guess, I think that might be hard to do."

"Why's that?" Sicilia asks. Frellman takes her shoulder and spins her around to see the conversation that Aarik is having.

"Because he seems to be tongue deep in another count looking for players for his house."

Aarik is indeed pressing against the count he had been speaking to a few moments earlier. They now exchange a passionate and deep kiss. Aarik pushes the man's body against the stonewall in the back corner, groping at the man's bald head and letting the man pull at Aariks butt.

"Aarik!" Sycilia shouts as she rips her brother off the count of house Crowder.

Aarik wipes his mouth, removing some of the remaining count on his chin. "Oh, hey sis."

"Don't hey sis me, you sissy."

"What's your problem? I'm doing what we came here to do."

"We came here to convince someone to let us rent an apartment, not help spread the next wave of Frolaxia."

"Do you have Frolaxia?" Count Crowder asks.

"No!" Aarik says quickly. He then turns to Sycilia, "Sycilia, believe it or not, I'm actually doing my part."

"How?"

"We were just celebrating, cause I signed up for the Scatterbattle tournament. We'll be playing for House Crowder, and when we win, we get the keys to his tower loft."

"But, I can't let you live there if you have the Faerie Fever," Crowder says.

"We don't have Frolaxia." Aarik turns back to the Count. "I'm clean, honey."

"Well isn't that great," Sycilia says. "Maybe if you weren't too busy making out with everyone in Valeward, you'd have checked in on me first."

"Why?"

Crowder leans toward Sycilia, "Do you have Frola–"

"Bring up Frolaxia one more time, Stewart," Aarik says sternly.

Sycilia eyes the count for a moment, then turns to Aarik. "Because I have just made an agreement with the Weis family, to play on their Scatterbattle duo. So we can move into their loft."

"Well, wait, but that's what I just did," Aarik says flabbergasted.

"I know." Sycilia tightens her lips, crosses her arms and stares her brother down. He's a smart guy, she knows this, he's probably smarter than her, but sometimes he's just so dumb.

"But you're doing the thing that I just did."

"Yeah." She thinks back to the last day she saw him before he left for the academy. He was shorter; they both were. His hair was short and under control. It didn't have the white fade. He was always a princely boy. He cried thinking of leaving; she didn't. She couldn't let herself break, she wouldn't let their parents see her in pain. Her heart broke that day, and she knew that his did too. But part of her became calloused from the pain, part of her hated him for leaving.

"We're going to be fighting against each other."

"That's correct," Sycilia says. Aarik runs his hands through his now long dreads, pulling at the skin on his face. He breathes in through his teeth, looking at the ground. "That's right, you dummy, if you had been smarter, you would have confirmed with me before you signed up with baldy mcbalderson over here,"

"I'm still royalty and can have you thrown in jail at a moment's notice," Crowder says.

Sycilia holds up her hands. "Right, sorry. Anyway, you think you're some kind of main character in a myth or something." She puts her finger in Aarik's chest. "And you can just do whatever you want, and I'll come tagging along. But I got news for you, I'm a main character, too."

"First of all, you can't have two main characters–that's not how stories work." Aarik pushes her finger away, remembering how strong she is.

"Yes you can," she retorts.

"That's why they're called 'main' characters. If you have more than one, then they're just characters." Before she can argue, Aarik continues, "And furthermore, I contrast what you're saying with deliberate scrutiny. It has been proposed that I might indeed be more inclined to lead us, as I'm the more eloquent and cranial."

"Are you trying to use smart words to intimidate me?"

"Indeed!"

"Your fancy words don't scare me, 'cause at the end of the day, I know I can shove them back in your mouth hole."

The entire royal court is now watching the debate with tuned ears. The waiters are overfilling glasses as their attention is completely absorbed by the scene.

"An ostentatious venture, I would observe, and a self deprecating one at that, as you prove yourself to be the ogre with your own lack of lexicon."

"You stop that high classing language right now." Sycilia points her finger at him again.

"Nay, m'lady."

"You stop that right now, or I'm gonna slap that grin right off your face."

"Indeed, it would bring me pleasure to witness you attempt--"

Slap!

A collective gasp fills the room. Aarik reels back from the impact. He is less in shock than the rest of the room, rubbing the hot cheek, but focuses his eyes on Sicilia's angry face.

"Your offer of a duel has been accepted," Aarik exclaims as he brings his chin up and literally looks down on her over his nose. "We shall see each other on the field of Scatterbattle. I for my House Crowder, and your House Weis."

Sycilia shakes her head. "You're such an ass."

The door to the Penny Lich bursts open. The tavern is in full lunch as the dock workers have made their way to the bar. They drink as though they don't mean to return to work, giving a little too much attention to Gwen and not enough to Brohn.

Decorations of the end of year celebration, Semperlunas, are strewn about the place. Ella has been drafted into the decorating committee by Gwen and Hadvar. Hadvar and Ella unpack the balls of colored paper he has had stored in the basement for some time.

Every eye in the tavern turns to see who's bursting through the door, only to see Sycilia and Aarik shoving each other as they gasp for air.

"Ella!" Sycilia shouts out, "I need your help!"

"Brohn, buddy!" Aarik runs over to the burly man. "You remember that night a while back, when I did that thing for you, and you said, 'I owe you one, Aarik,' and I said, 'Don't worry about it, bud, I gotchu.' Do you remember that? When that happened?"

"Yeah, I remember."

"Well, I lied, you should have worried about it, cause now I'm calling in that favor."

"Aarik is being an ass, as per usual," Sycilia says. "He went and made out with sir fancy pants and got himself admitted to the Scatterbattle tournament, and then I was all like, 'uh, hold up, I just did that but with a different person, and without putting my tongue down his throat,' and then he was all like, 'duh, duh, I'm just a horny pansexual that will sleep with anything that moves, and I don't actually want to help you.'"

"I said no such thing!" Aarik turns away from Brohn. "I would never box myself into a specific sexuality."

"That's what you have a problem with?" Sycilia shoots back.

"What's going on?" Hadvar shouts out.

"I already told you," Sycilia says. "This fool over here is ruining our only chance at not sleeping in the gutter tonight."

"I'm doing what needs to be done, and then you got all uppity 'cause for once you had to rely on someone else, which is impossible for you."

"How dare you!" Sycilia finally pulls her sword out and begins moving toward her brother. A missing finger wouldn't kill him. They could heal it back on, and then she can cut it off again. Heck, with Elliot's skills, she might just cut off his di–

"Enough!" Hadvar stands between the twins and his stern look stops Sycilia in her tracks. "Lunch is over. Everyone back to work."

The tavern is quiet for a moment, while the dock workers and sailors watch the scene. "That means now!" Hadvar shouts again. A tremor rocks the room and every workman stands up and makes their way out. They mumble about needing a nap or the barmaid's hand in marriage, but they quickly empty the tavern. The Penny Lich crew stands in awe of the power demonstrated.

"How did you do that?" Aarik asks.

"I pour their drinks, if I decide to stop–"

"Power move, nice," Aarik says.

"What's going on between you two?"

"We went to the royal court, like Elliot recommended we do," Sycilia starts, "and while we were mingling with the royal houses, I was able to strike a deal with the Weis family to get a two bedroom dockside loft, built for literal royalty."

"Oh that sounds lovely," Gwen says.

"Right?" Sycilia acknowledges Gwen's input. "In order to make this deal I had to take my attention off this animal for like five minutes, and in that time he went and ruined everything."

"No." Aarik points. "I made my own deal. I didn't

just stand around like a good boy and let you do everything. Geez, you're just like our dad. The second I'm in any way an inconvenience you freak out and then blame me for your tantrum."

"How dare you!?" Sycilia flashes back to the moment she was introduced to Henderson, his slicked back hair, his bright eyes, his sly smile. She remembers the look on her dad's face: hope, expectation, duty. She knew right then and there that she was going to break his heart the way hers had been broken when Aarik left. She knew that she was going to ruin his plans, then Henderson took her hand. It's not Henderson's face, it's Hadvar. They pull their hair back the same way.

"Sycilia, please. I know this is frustrating,"

"Infuriating!" she shouts.

"Entertaining," Brohn says from the seat he's taken. He throws back an ale left behind.

"I can't believe you would compare me to the man who gave you everything, and tried to give me away. I can't believe you would suggest that I would pick and choose between my family and my honor. You know what, you can have your duel. I'll see you on the field, and when I beat you in the tournament, and you're homeless and have nothing, then maybe you'll realize that dad couldn't give you everything. Somethings you have to fight for, and that's what I'm best at." She pushes past Aarik, making her way toward the door. "Ella, get your things. We got some training to do."

"I would love to, but I'm still not sure what's happening."

"What's happening is you're my best friend, and your job is to help me beat the shit out of my brother. Let's go, dern it!" With that Ella bashes through a table and chair on her way out of the tavern. Ella grabs her jacket, and makes her way past Aarik. She stops on the other side of him, then turns around.

"I have to do this, 'cause I'm her best friend. You know that right?" Ella says.

"I do."

"Good luck."

"You too," Aarik says a half second before Ella spits on his face. The saliva smacks him in the forehead and his head moves back on instinct.

"Screw you, pig!" Ella screams. She then stomps her heel into Aarik's foot, and runs out the door.

"Why!?" Aarik shouts as she leaves. Aarik recovers and turns to Brohn.

Brohn is now eating the abandoned turkey leg while leaning back in his chair and chuckling at the scene. "I still have no idea what's happening."

"You've never played Scatterbattle before?" Aarik asks Brohn. The two men stand in a field, a large park surrounded by the bustling streets of Valeward, and its multi-story buildings. The field, The Daughters of Evergreen Park, is maintained by the local druid circle, though they rarely employ magic like their kin from outside the kingdom. Some of the higher ranked druids are given small allowances of magic to help with growth and healing tasks. The last real druid to step foot on the perfectly manicured grass was one of the two Daughters of Evergreen.

The two sisters had made it a point to turn the scene of a terrible tragedy into that of a great monument to the lost. They placed massive stones in the ground, carving the names of those that had lost their lives in the Turncoat Conflicts into them. In the two hundred years or so since they built the park, the names had begun to erode and fill with moss. They were well-worn reminders of a people that lost their lives in the Turncoat Conflicts, the reign of the Virgil Empire, and the Valeward Revolution.

Now goats wander the park and eat grass, the druids their shepherds. Honey Bees float about pollinating the various blocks of colorful flowers. The Circle of the Park Druids are more proficient with clippers than ancient magics, and rather than take on the form of a beast as the myths of old priests would do, these acolytes of nature are more inclined to shepherd them.

Aarik and Brohn stand in a section of the park where two large rocks provide adequate privacy, without cutting them off from the beauty of well-groomed park. Aarik holds a large wooden beam, its bottom sharpened and pointed at the dirt. Brohn in his great strength brings a wooden hammer down and smashes the piller into the ground. With a few swift smacks, the pole is set in place, rising up from the ground to Aarik's chest.

"Nope," Brohn says as he leans on the hammer. "I made money for my foster parents when I was a child. Didn't have time for games."

"This isn't just a game, Brohn. This is Scatterbattle."

"You say that like it's important to me, and yet I feel nothing."

"You must be dead inside. This is the game of royalty. The sport of kings."

"Sounds pretentious."

"Exactly!" Aarik grabs a second pole and readies 50 yards away. Brohn follows and prepares to bring the hammer down. "While this area is a bit smaller than an actual scatter field, it will work for the purpose of training."

"I still don't know what we're doing." WHACK! "I mean, this seems kinda like defacement of public property." WHACK! "And what do we do with these things?" WHACK! The pillar stands.

"First of all, don't be a little newb, there is no such thing as public space. Everything is owned by the royal families. This place is owned by the Evergreens. The Mistress is an Evergreen, I think. And since we work for the Magecore, we have every right to use it accordingly."

"We work for the Magecore? I thought the whole point of starting the guild was for Elliot and Moses to get away from the Magecore."

"Anyone who does magic is controlled by the Magecore; that's literally what they do. It's an oppressive state mandate that helps codify their necessity and push for greater control over the people. Secondly, I'm gonna teach you everything you need to know, right now."

"Uh, ok." Brohn looks around without complete confidence. Or any confidence.

"It's simple. Two teams of two compete to collect as many points as possible before the three rounds of play are over. Whoever has the most points when the final round is finished, wins the game. To get points, a slug from the one team must hit the buttress of the opposing team. That pole you just smacked. The magician is normally responsible for this, as they have direct control of the slugs on the field, allowing them to throw, deflect, defend, distract, and ultimately make contact with the buttress. The opposing team is using their slugs to do the same.

"All the while the pug is on the field running offense for the team. They use either a bokken, staff, or club to fight off both the other team's pug and the slugs. Their ultimate aim is twofold: distract the opposing magician enough that their own magician can land a few slugs on the buttress, gaining them a few points; and then to end the game by landing their weapon of choice on the buttress. This will not only end the round, but add a certain amount of points to the final tally. That is decided by this location here." Aarik stops talking for a moment to take a breath, and places a pillar in the middle of the two others.

"This is the duel pillar. To cross into the enemy's territory, a pug must make contact with the duel pillar. If a pug is able to get to the duel pillar, make contact, cross the scrimmage line first and hit the opponent's buttress without being knocked down, then that team will be rewarded twenty points. If the pug is the second one over the line of scrimmage, their end of round points are cut in half. So instead of twenty extra, it'd be ten, obviously."

"Obvioulsy," Brohn says, obviously lost.

"And if a pug is knocked down and is warped to their buttress for reset, then they will also halve the end of round points. Potentially a twenty point extra, possibly down to a five point extra. See? Super easy."

"Ok," Brohn says as he thinks through the rules just dumped on him. He picks up one of the balls covered in magic runes, he looks at it carefully, then sees the gloves that Aarik is putting on, a bit of technology mixed with ancient runes. "So, this is–" He holds onto the thought as he questions all the rules, "-- a slug."

Aarik breathes out in disappointment, activating the gloves with magic. The slug in Brohn's hand glows, and suddenly shoots into Aarik's hand, "Yes, Brohn. Ball is slug."

"This place is dope!" Sycilia says as she falls on

the sofa looking out at Valeward Lake. The apartment she's in is truly made for royalty, with wood paneling, a great hearth stove, an open room concept with a kitchenette, and a small library. Two small staircases rise up on the wall where the front door is built. The stairs each lead to a door about six feet off the ground, into separate bedrooms.

"Do you have a preference on which bedroom you want?" Ella asks from one of the staircases.

"Nope," Sycilia says.

"Good, you get this one." Ella comes out of the room and jumps down to the main floor.

"This room is really nice," Gwen says from the other bedroom door balcony.

"Ella, what's going on in that room?" Sycilia asks, hopping up and running to the room Ella just left. Ella walks to the back door, and out on the balcony.

"You don't want that room, Ella?" Gwen asks.

"Nope."

"Gross!" Sycilia comes stumbling out.

"What? What is it?" Gwen asks. She runs down the stairs, around the room, then back up the other staircase. Sycilia offers her hand to give permission for entry, a sly smile on her face. Gwen's wonder is squashed as she walks through the doorway. Paintings of erotic poses hang from every wall. A bed made in the shape of a heart. Lanterns cast a dimmed and magical watery light. And a mirror hangs, attached to the ceiling above the bed.

"Oh come on," Gwen says, beginning to laugh.

"No," Sycilia begins laughing too. "No, this is awful. It's not funny."

"Looks like Aster's bedroom. Are you ready for the fire lord to arrive?"

"Stop, no. I can't live like this. I can't sleep in this

room."

"From what it looks like," Gwen continues to laugh, "it wasn't made for sleeping in."

"You said you didn't care," Ella says looking up at the ceiling of the living space. She turns her head like a cat watching prey.

"That's before I knew that this room was covered in lube and a deadman's spooge," Sycilia says.

"Fine, the other room."

"Also, don't say spooge. It's gross," Gwen says.

"Wait, you're fine sleeping in here?" Sycilia asks Ella as she makes her way to the living room.

"I guess, but I probably won't spend much time in there."

"Where are you gonna spend your time?" Gwen asks, leaning on the handrail. Ella smiles at her and points up. The two ladies look up and see on the tall ceiling a small trap door. As they both take a second to realize what it is, the sound of a crossbow releases, and a bolt snaps into the wood next to the door. Attached to the bolt is the steel wire that Recky used in the Sandren Temple.

Ella quickly climbs up the rope, twenty or so feet into the air, unlatches the door and lets it swing open. She then propels herself forward enough to get her legs in the space. The woman pulls herself up and disappears into the dark space above their heads.

"Do you think she's coming back?" Gwen asks.

"I genuinely have no idea."

Suddenly a rope ladder descends down from the trap door and smacks the floor of their living room. "This is a dream come true," Ella says with a lack of emotion that leaves an odd feeling in the two ladies below. "It's a low ceiling space, with a single window. This is the only way up, and it has enough room for my bed roll."

"You want to sleep up there!?" Sycilia asks.

"Yeah, this is kinda perfect. I'm a weird person, Sycilia, I don't know if you figured that one out."

"I was starting to get the impression."

"And I don't generally feel comfortable in rooms like normal people. I certainly wouldn't like sleeping in that goop room."

"Worse, so much worse," Gwen says.

"Up here, I'm protected, hidden and safe."

"If you help me win this loft, you can sleep wherever you want." Sycilia watches as Gwen starts climbing the rope ladder up to the attic. "We'll just need to find someone to fill the third room." She smiles as Ella grabs Gwen's arm and hoists her up into the new bedroom.

"So this is it!" Aarik says as he walks Brohn through the door of the apartment. "Crowder says we can stay here for the weekend as we play in the tournament. Pretty sweet, eh?"

"This is nice, yeah," Brohn says looking around.

The Crowder house looks out at the city lights, stone floor, stone walls, and stone windows. Well, the frames are stone, obviously the rest of the windows are made of Hallowed Coast Sand, melted down and forged into window panes by the plain monks. A name of which they earned, not for making window planes, but because they hail from the plains of Tamed Yonder.

"Cool windows," Brohn says.

"Yeah, I know, right?" Aarik says. "So–"

"So?"

"So, if you help me win this thing, I have an extra bedroom, all for you, my guy."

"Oh, Aarik, that's awesome. I'm happy to help you win. I mean, we drank King's Casket together, I'm with you through anything."

"Awesome. I figure you'll take the lower room over there, and I'll take the master room, 'cause, well to be honest, I think I'm gonna utilize my room a little more than you might."

Brohn looks uncomfortable, realizing he needs to back peddle. He throws his hands up and tries to interrupt Aarik.

"And then we can throw parties and be like, huh, yeah we won this place in a tournament. Do you know how many chicks we're gonna get with that line? Wait, you like girls? Or guys? I've never thought to ask."

"I uh, girls, I guess. But look man, I'm happy to help but I don't--"

"You don't have to worry, you're not imposing at all. I want you to live here. It's all good. It's my gift to you."

"No, Aarik, I don't want to live here."

Aarik keeps walking around, talking about their parties and breakfast foods when he stops. He turns, confusion running over his face. He had misheard, of course he had misheard. Someone would be crazy to not want to live in this place. Look at all the windows.

"I beg your pardon?" Aarik asks.

"I'm actually pretty happy with where I'm at, so, let's win this, but let's win this for you, eh?"

"But look at all the windows."

The first day of the tournament wakes with the players of the games. The players make their way to the gulch where Valeward's castle rests. They stretch and practice on the Scatterbattle arena, built into the same area as the royal houses and mansions of Valeward's elite. A simple walk from the front door for the prestigious. A climb of dedication to the top of the Valeward hills for the townsfolk.

Three pillars rest on the field: two at the ends of the arena and one in the middle. Each has a circle around them, and a line passing through the middle circle and pillar.

Most seats are on the balconies of the royal houses and decks of the great halls. Then around the actual field, bleachers are erected for the common folk. Stones laid in the ground represent the entirety of the field, with runes carved into them. Those that have seen a game before know that the runes create an invisible blockade that the slugs can't pass through.

The pugs for each team find friendly sparring partners and test their leather armor. Like rams clashing, they come down on eachother; some fall, some draw, some plough so hard through their competition it scares other pugs.

Magicians wear the traditional mage's cap, reinforced with metal and hard leather, an extra bit of fabric hanging from the tip to give it the whimsical look magician's are known for. They wear padded cloaks and hold gloves for channeling. Attuned to the specific slug for their team, the channeling gloves are personal for each magician. The only similarity is the channeling band and the resonating orb placed in it. Some wear long gloves where the band wraps around the elbow. Some wear the band around their knuckles, the resonating orb punching the slugs into motion. Most have the orb in their palm, so as to feel the ball in their hands when they reach out for it.

"So you can't cast any spell except control with those on?" Gwen asks, watching Ella put the black leather gloves on.

"Yeah," Ella says. She finishes pulling them tight, then activates the resonating orb, a roughly cut gem that glows the same gold color as the slugs around her. They all let off a thrum. "This technology goes back to when the magcore first handicapped the wizards and mages of Valeward. Back before the Valeward Revolution."

"I thought the Magecore started after the revolution."

"They were named the Magecore after, but the department still existed. One of the dominions of the Hallow Conclave, so they had one of the seats in the senate."

"I don't understand. What does the dominion of the Conclave cares about this sport."

"There is a sect of the Conclave that the Virgil Empire embraces, called the Pact. It is a god that holds the gods accountable"

"Wouldn't that be the job of like the God of Order?" Gwen asks, grabbing the magician's helmet.

"What happens when Order takes over and destroys chaos, wildness, and chance? Where would the world evolve without turmoil? This Pact god, and its deity are the only ones that keep the world in balance. So when Virgil took over, they found that magic had run rampant, not to mention the elves to the north were beginning to have too much influence on us. So they enacted the Pact deity to help find balance. The deity knew that he couldn't stop magic, but he also knew people were inclined toward entertainment. He worked with the Study of Arts, the Techmages, to create these. They transform every bit of magic I might cast into control over things that resonate with this orb. It was great. The Scatterbattle was born, and people with magic in their blood were given a chance to perform and earn a living. They were no longer slaughtered and massacred."

"My Conclave, that's awful."

"Being taken from your family, trained, fed, and treated like a champion was a whole heck of a lot better than being run through with a blade or having your throat cut as a baby. But of course, people suck, and as time went on, the channeling magic proved useful for manual labor, moving things, building things, heck even with the right resignation orbs, you could build a small army of channelers. So the mageslave was created. If you showed any sign of magic in you, your parents had the right to sell you off to Scatterbattle teams, or the farmer down the road."

"This is getting so depressing. I'm starting to regret asking." Gwen puts the helmet on Ella's head.

"Most people do," Ella says then continues, "But remember the small army of channelers thing? Well, when the revolution happened, that was a big part of it. Magicians who had never been given proper training in magic, other than channeling, could aid in fighting off Virgil. In return, they would earn freedom."

"But the Magecore is still a thing. You said it started in Virgil, but they're still controlling people with magic. "

"Traditions in culture are hard to kill, it takes time, it takes an understanding of how people can accept things. Nothing changes too slowly. It's been a couple hundred years now, and sure the Magecore still runs anything magical, but they also help people find jobs. The temples, the firemages, scholars, even Scatterbattle. They do the work of helping people when they can, and punishing people when they think they need to. Even this game, they push for it as a way to help us remember the channelers who fought for Valeward's indiependence. When I put on this glove, I become like those that gave their lives, and I know that I have the strength to fight for what I want."

Gwen smiles at Ella's sentiment. Ella stares at the resonating orb, thinking about the magic that flows in the glove. The past of magic in her valley, and the Pact that brought them here.

"And we pugs just want to smack someone in the face," Sycilia says as she comes out of her dressing room, full gear, and a bokken in hand, "Especially when that person is my entitled brat for a brother." She brings the bokken down and slices the air.

Sycilia brings the wooden sword down as she enters the duel pillar circle and smacks the opponent pug in the face, keeping him from touching the pillar with his sword. The center of the field is busy with their duel, both fighting for control, trying to be the first to pass the line of scrimmage. Sycilia wears the gold of the Weis house, while her opponent wears the blue of the Denier Family. The sound of their wooden blades cracking is covered by the roar of applause as the first game begins. Streamers and flashes of skyfire explode; cheering and general celebration resound from the stands. Men seated above on porches make bets and talk amongst themselves in very important and highly educated diction.

Ella trades slugs with the other magician. The blue balls start testing Ella's ability to move quickly while covering her post. She sends several probing shots herself to see if the other magician is up to the task, and he is. He deflects several incoming missiles, and when Ella uses a trick throw to get him unarmed for a moment, he takes the third incoming slug with his forearms and slides back a few feet.

Ella realizes that the best way to get her opponent off kilter is if Sycilia can pull his attention, so Ella changes targets. While still defending her own pillar, she begins to throw spare slugs down the center field toward the opponent pug.

Sycilia, still unable to tap the duel pillar, finally lets the opponent slash at her, moving at the last second to spin and strike at the pillar. She can feel the wind of his strike blow past her, and she feels the edge of the opponent's blunted weapon make contact on her cape. Spinning and bringing her bokken out, ready to land it on the duel pillar and move on, suddenly a gold slug slams into her back, knocking her off balance.

She lands, looks back, glaring at Ella. "The Hell-realm was that?"

Ella gave Sycilia a thumbs up, hoping that was the right response..

The blue pug smacks the pillar and begins toward the gold pillar. Unwilling to let the moment pass, Sycilia throws the Bokken so it spins and catches the man's feet. Tripping him up before he leaves the center circle.

Sycilia rolls and pulls the man's feet back toward her, grabbing her blade and smacking the pillar. She then rolls backward and pushes herself out of the circle on the blue side.

"Gold takes the scrimmage!" an announcer says from the side of the rink. He speaks into a rod that booms his voice across the entire gully. "Looks like we have a scrappy start to this year's season folks."

A red slug flies through the air as the start horn blares. Aarik, ready for the strike, brings his green slug up like a shield and deflects, then tracks the other two slugs inbound and does the geometry in his head.

His fingers pulse in electric excitement, then shift upward. Two green slugs follow his command and streak toward the red missiles high above the duel pillar.

As the green intercepts the red slugs, they collide and the red's path is changed into a sharper downward arc. It tags the red pug and throws him off balance. Brohn takes the opportunity and swings his club at the man's face, knocking him down. Without a second's hesitation, Brohn barrels through the line of scrimmage. His large frame and strong grasp on his club ready him for the beating. He smiles as he feels the weak slugs bounce from his weapon.

The red magician focuses on the ox charging toward him and takes all attention off offense. He pulls several slugs near him, creating piles on either side of him. They continue to float out of the underground portal; when one is taken, a new one replaces it, levitating upward in a glow of red. The magician takes them as they appear, amassing his artillery.

When Brohn is close enough, the magician, with a sly grin, sends several of the slugs into the air, high, straight up. Brohn watches them for a second, and when he looks back to question the magician, two slugs smash into his face. His rush is broken, and he steadies himself from the hits, seeing through stars. By the time his eyes adjust, two more slugs lock onto him, but he perries one, and dodges the other. Thinking he has the timing down, he squares up again, and takes a step forward, only to be met with two more. The first is high, for his face. He deflects it, but it takes all his vision to do so, and he doesn't see the second coming for his gut. It bends him over as it rails into him. Then a third at the same level, where his head now sits. He takes the hit and begins falling backward.

With all his fortitude, he pushes the club in his

hands down into the ground to steady himself.

"Don't fall." Aarik's instructions ring in his ear. "Whatever you do, do not go down."

The club takes hold on the fresh grass, and he pushes himself in a back flip over it. It's at this point he remembers the slugs sent directly up. They are now falling down toward him. As Brohn comes to the peak of his flip, he's hit with two falling slugs, enchanted by the magician's extra pull downward. Two more are thrown by the opposing mage. As Brohn hits the ground and registers the pain of being a pug, his vest glows and then sings in magic.

Suddenly he's out of time and space again, and he hates it. An odd image of space, endless space, then a great inverted pyramid, then a woman with tattoos. Then he's back at the green pillar. Aarik is defending the buttress from the red pug, while preparing to defend from the incoming slugs.

"You fell!?" Aarik shouts without taking his eyes off the dodging aggressor.

"I tried not to."

"Hey, hey!" Aarik shouts. "You have to tap our buttress before you enter the field again."

"Oh, ok."

"Hurry up and take this guy down. I've landed a couple shots on their pillar, but you need to take some pressure off."

Brohn taps the pillar with his club then jets toward the pug. The man is defending himself from an onslaught of slugs. Aarik gives Brohn the cover he needs to close the gap, as several red slugs try to strike him. By the time Brohn is within range, the red pug readies himself for a fight.

The man strikes first as Brohn approaches, rolling toward him and slashing at Brohn's feet. Brohn jumps and flips in the air, a feat Aarik is taken aback by. The size of Brohn betrays his agility and helps keep the red fighter off balance. Brohn, now standing behind the red pug, spins around and slams his club into his opponents knees. This takes the man off his feet, his face cracks on the ground. His body falls flat, and his vest sings its tune, then the body sucks into a small vortex and reemerges next to the red buttress.

"Holy frick frack!" Aarik says with a smile. A moment of peace as the red magician checks on his partner.

"You're not gonna shoot the piller?" Brohns asks.

"Professional courtesy. You laid that guy out."

"I just did what you told me to."

"No, listen." Aarik points his finger up. Brohn listens to the crowd. Together they chant.

"Green Smasher! Green Smasher! Green Smasher!"

"That's pretty cool, eh?" Brohn says with a smile.

"Literal goosebumps. Chills, bro," Aarik says. He then raises his hand to the red magician. A green slug flies up to the middle pillar and holds in the air. Aarik's hand glows as he holds the ball in place. "We were first to cross, twenty points, but you fell, so we have ten end of round points, they were second and fell so they have five. Make sense?"

"No."

"Good, I've hit a few times, but so have they, which means we might be closer than we think. So I want you to end this as soon as possible. They only get one courtesy from me. He knows how hard you hit, and if they continue to play, then his life is in his hands."

"What are you saying?" Brohn asks as he stands next to Aarik.

"When they hit my slug, I want you to break

them." Aarik says. Brohn can't help but feel nostalgia rush over him. The feeling of being a child and knowing that he was more powerful than the other opponents. Brohn doesn't lose.

"Green Smasher! Green Smasher!" the crowd chants. Brohn grimaces in the realization that he loves this, soaking in the memory of blood. He tightens his grip and watches as the red team readies themselves. Then a red ball flies into the air and knocks into the green slug.

"Go get 'em green smasher," Aarik says, and Brohn takes off like an arrow.

"Well folks, it's been quite the day, I'll tell ya what. We've seen games of Scatterbattle before, but it seems like the great houses of Valeward have gone out of their way to bring us the cream of the crop this year. No one is surprised by the ladies representing the Weis house, donning the gold and making it gleam brighter. These two have absolutely dominated their fields as they prove once again that the Weis family is not one to be underestimated.

"Their magician, a young lady known as Ella Monroe, seems to have a hyper fixation on decimating the opposing pugs as they try to make their way toward the gold buttress. She's not too bad at those long shots to gain a few points, but as we saw in the match against the Gerell bronze duo, it's when her opponents get a little too close that she seems to strike like a viper, taking out the bronze pug's legs, and landing several slugs on his face before he had the grace to fall.

"But the true star has to be her partner. Gold pug Sycilia Willowmight looks as though she's got a grudge with every unfortunate opponent that dares step in front of her. As they make their way into the semifinals bracket, it seems as though her fire burns a little brighter. The speed and focus of her blade speaks to the endless hours she's spent perfecting her art. She pulled her team through to the finals, with her dedication and unflinching resolve in the face of much more experienced and highly expected duos.

"I had the opportunity to sit down with our semifinalist as she prepared to leave for the day. Stay tuned to your scrolls for that interview coming up after a couple words from our patrons."

"Now open! The Gerell Museum of Fine Arts and Music! Are you a fan of tales told by bards in the tavern or on the lonely roads? Looking to see the history of the craft of storycraft? Come down to the Gerell Museum of Fine Arts and Music! The Gerell family has been collecting pieces of Valeward and Yonder Valley history for decades, preserving it for future generations. In hopes of helping the next Indriq Olenor find their voice. Heck, we even have the Olenor melodica on display (all Olenor related products are sold with permission from Evergreen and Reed enterprises).

"Are you a farmer with a plot of land on the edge of town that seems to be constantly attacked by bandits or gremlins? Are you in need of someone to investigate a missing family heirloom or family member? Have you upset a hag and/or fey creature and now need a way out of a bloodpact? Well look no further! The Penny Lich guild is here for you, even when the Magecore doesn't have time for you. If you need a little extra muscle, divine intervention, or just someone to talk to, we have just the people for you. Just come down to the Penny Lich and ask for Moses Summer-hill."

"I'm sitting with Sycilia, a beauty of a pug, I must say. Her eyes focus with a piercing fury that I can only assume strikes fear into the hearts of the others on the field. Her great arms are toned with muscle and covered in a warm undertone of brown skin. As she sits in comfortable clothes, I can hardly believe that this enchantress could be the same woman that smashed a bukken into the chest of an opponent so hard that he vomited on the spot."

"Well, that's not really what I was going for. I just wanted to him to stop giving Ella a hard time, ya know?"

"I do, and thank you so much for taking time to talk with me."

"Of course, thanks for that kind introduction."

"Tell us, Sycilia, you've come into the tournament with such ferocity and passion, what drives that?"

"Well I just wanted to find a place to live 'cause I got kicked out of the tavern I was staying in. So I went to the royal courts to ask around, met up with Count Weis, one thing led to another, and here I am."

"There are plenty of duos working out some deals with a patron, but it seems like there's something more."

"I, uh, well, to be honest I spent a few years in trouble with the law while I lived in Valley Gate. I learned to survive and fight for everything. I guess I go into the field with the same ferocity as I did trying to stay alive back in the day."

"Some say it's no coincidence that you're not holding back, and your brother, Aarik Willowmight, is also in this tournament. Do you have any comments on that?"

"No. No, I don't. Not really. No. It just, I feel like it's unsportsmanlike for me to talk about it here, ya know? 'Cause really it's a personal issue, that I guess is getting dragged out into the public eye, since we're doing this tournament. So, no. I don't have anything to say about it. It's just, like, this is so him, right? Like, he could have just been on my team, could have just followed me for once. Instead, he had to go be his normal sleazy self and do his own thing, and I'm left here, alone, fending for myself, trying to figure out how to do this all without him, all because he wanted to be a pathfinder on his own."

"Oh, well, yeah, I guess if you don't want to talk about it--"

"And you know what? I'm doing just fine, ok? I'm good. I don't need him. I never did. I have my girl, Ella, and Gwen, and the Weis house backing me up, and I plan on taking this blade and slapping him in the face with it so hard that our mama feels it."

"Oh, ok. Wow, that's a lot for someone who didn--"

"So I'm coming for you Aarik. I'm coming for your stupid little magician face. You see Ol' Slappy here? That's my sword, I call it Ol' Slappy now, and it's gonna get shoved right up your--"

"Oh, ok. That's quite enough, I think. Stay scrolling 'cause after these quick patrons, we'll be talking to Crowder's green team magician, Aarik Willowmight."

"You're gonna talk to him? You tell him something for me, you tell him I know he wet the bed until he was--"

Smooth. Decadent. Capable of setting an entire swarm of spiders on fire. These are all things that my great great great grandfather described when he first created Raggamuffin Moonshine. First distilled in the basement of the Penny Lich in Haberdashery Woods, we are now a kingdom-wide operation that takes pride in the small town feel of our goblin run brewery. From Goblin Ale to Norbang Mead, to our newest concoction–he pre-bottled Blue River Ale–e'll have just the drink for you. Ragamuffin Brewing: Goblin Owned, Heroes Welcome.

If you or a loved one have been exhibiting signs of magical ability, it is your duty to King and Country to submit yourself to the ever watchful eye of the Magecore. Over seeing the safe practices of magic users in Valeward proper for over two hundred years. Don't let yourself become the problem; train to become the solution. Join the Magecore.

"I'm here with Aarik Willowmight, magician of the Crowder green team, and I have to say, I've very quickly become a huge fan of yours."

"Appreciate it, but uh, just a heads up its pronounced Air Rick."

"Really? This whole time I was saying Are Reek."

"Yeah, I get that a lot. Some people even call me Air Rik."

"How's that different from what you just said?"

"They drop the c."

"Oh, uh, ok."

"So how does this work?"

"No, please, don't touch that; it's a magic scroll."

"Magic? That's so cool. How does it work? I'm guessing it writes everything we say?"

"Yeah, my subscribers have a scroll at home and this shows up live on the Scrollcast."

"Amazing."

"I'll tell you what's amazing, you and your teammate, the Green Smasher, Brohn Meyers. Coming out of nowhere, underdogs in every match up, and you came in blazing. That first round smash for Brohn set the tone for the rest of the day."

"Brohn's a great player, strong and fast, and I have to give him all the credit. I'm just out there to have fun, and you know, win."

"I would say so. In your next few matches, we watched as Brohn cut down foes like trees in the forest, punishing just about anyone that dared to look him in the eye. I have to wonder if his time as an orphan pushed him into the life of violence?"

"Brohn's an orphan?"

"According to our research, he was born and raised here in Valeward, and spent a lot of time in the foster program. Some even suspect his involvement in an underground betting ring. But whatever got him here, it's a boone to you, am I right?"

"I guess. Yea. I mean, I would hate to know that he's doing all this and it's killing him a little, you know? I want to win, but I don't want to win that badly."

"Well, It seems like you want to win very badly. In this semifinal match you won by taking out both the pug and the magician at once, an amazingly focused attack that has never been seen before. You have earned the title of ring sniper. How do you feel about that?"

"I've been working my whole life to be as good as I am. I was taken to the finest school in the kingdom and learned from the best. I can't let them down."

"Truly royal blood in this magician. And are you worried about your sister at all?"

"Nope. She's a lot of bluster, but not a lot of bite."

"Well, her bite sent a man to the temple for reconstruction on his head."

"Oh, Conclave. She messed up his face that bad?"

"Not that head."

"Shhheeeeee."

"I have to say, it's nice to see a competitor who is as gifted as you are, and yet calm and confident. It must come from the lifestyle that comes from living with royalty and comfort in your younger days. Competitor's like your sister have struggled for so long that every win is a win for their entire being. If they lose, they see it as a fundamental flaw in themselves. Where someone like you knows there will always be another match, another chance to win. And I think that confidence can give someone like you nerves of steel when facing down a raging bull like the gold team."

"Yeah, I guess, hmm. I guess I never really thought about it that way, ya know."

"You ok?"

"Hmm, what?"

"Well you're looking off into the middle distance there, lights shining in your eyes like thoughts swirling in your head, illuminating a sudden epiphany."

"Oh, no, sorry. It's just the Ragamuffin Mead I downed before I did this interview. Ok, slug mouth, time for me to make my escape."

"Well ok. And as Aarik Willowmight, the magician for Crowder, stumbles off in a drunken stupor, surely off to celebrate a victorious day, we shall say good night. Remember to watch your scroll tomorrow for play by play commentary on a Scatterbattle match for the ages. Who will win? who will get the apartment promised to them? Find out next time on Scattered Plays Scrollcast."

Aarik sits at the grand table of the Crowder apartment and looks out the window at the city. The lights in the morning darkness look like spirits in the void. He chews on his tongue as he watches the morning guard take their route, like ants from this view. They light torches and lamps for the new day. Some stalls begin their set up for the day, men and women working for a living, selling bread and buying meat from hunters and stacking fish. Gross stinky fish.

A baker down the hill sets up his stall outside his bakery, the scent of bread permeating the square. His wife comes out with several new loafs. He takes them and kisses her, then goes back to work. The guards on duty walk on, illuminated by their torches. Aarik's keen eyes watch as they're about to disappear, believing they are unseen by prying eyes. They hold hands and walk on.

Aarik looks around the apartment surrounded by stone. Stone table, floor, and walls; everything is rock. Except for the flap jacks. The flap jacks are good. He takes a bite of one and closes his eyes in pleasure. He squishes his face in approval of the breakfast treat, nodding his head. After opening his eyes he looks at the flapjack on his plate, then up at the stacks and stacks of flapjacks on the table. He expected Brohn to be here. He expected Crowder to stay through the night. He expected to not be alone.

He stands up, pushing the sickly sweet carbs away from him and moves toward the window. He has been here before. Alone. He's been this way his entire life. He blames it on the world, on others, but at the end of the day, or rather the beginning of the day, he's the one that pushed the most important person in his life away. He could try to find solace in making her stronger, making her better. But then he would be no better than his father.

The moment that thought hooks into his mind, his eyes widen in revelation. Brohn walks in through the front door.

"I'm sorry I was late," Brohn starts as he makes his way to the table. "I got lost on my way here. Do you know how confusing the Highland District is?" Brohn sits down and immediately begins pouring sap syrup on his massive plate of flapjacks. "I'm actually very glad I got here before you left, 'cause I've been looking forward to this stack for some time. I heard Gwen was making breakfast for the gold team, and I was tempted, only tempted mind you, to head over there and get some of that. But then I thought, no, no, I'm obligated to eat Aarik's flapjacks. Being best friends and all."

Aarik turns around and Brohn stops from taking his first bite. "Oh, Aarik, that came out wrong, man. I mean to say, I'm super excited to give up breakfast with a large number of my friends made by the best cook I know, to come eat these cold pancakes with just you. Ok, that sounded sarcastic, but I didn't mean it like that,"

"Put that flapjack down!" Aarik shouts, pointing at Brohn. "Go get Gwen, bring her to the tournament field."

"Why?"

Aarik's eyes narrow. "And tell her to bring Potsticker."

"You still haven't answered my question," Brohn says, still sitting at the table with his pancakes.

"What?" Aarik asks, snapping out of his concentration.

"I asked you why, and you just gave me more of a demand, you didn't actually answer my question."

"Oh, I was being dramatic, you know. Saving the

explanation for later, after you've done what I ask."

"Ok, but, what if Gwen asks why? What am I supposed to say? 'Cause Aarik says so? That's probably not gonna fly, and you think Elliot is just gonna let us take Potsticker? He's the guard--"

"Stop, stop, stop, just come on. Just go get them; I'll explain at the field."

"No. I don't think I'm gonna do that."

"Could you please, for one second stop being such a stick in the mud, GAWH!"

"Aarik, what's going on?"

"I, uh, I just, I feel like. I feel like I need to cancel the tournament," Aarik says, giving up and sitting down at the table.

"What? What are you talking about?"

"I was going to use Potsticker to cause the Valeward Volcano to spew some black smoke, and scare everyone into thinking it was gonna explode while you and I face Sycilia and Ella, and instead they cancel everything."

Brohn looks at Aarik for a moment, then at the table. His eyes dart back and forth while he slowly brings a pancake to his mouth. He chews on it as he explores Aarik's idea in his head. A stern look smears on his face as the sweet sap smears over his beard. He wipes away the sugar, but the frown sticks.

"Are you #@&ing insane?" Brohn says in all seriousness.

"What?"

"If you did that, it would cause the entire city to shut down. Entire families would be upheaved and moved. People could and most likely would die in the chaos. The entire government would be thrown into hysteria, and crime would be rampant. And you would do all this, because you don't want to lose to your sister?"

"It's not that, Brohn! I wouldn't do all that, just to make sure I don't lose. I would do it so I don't have to apologize to her." As Aarik finishes his words a flapjack smacks him in the face. It flew through the air so fast, and out of nowhere, he had no chance to avoid it. The sappy carb attack sticks to his face, and he reels back. As he pulls the pancake from his eyes, he sees a second breaded disc incoming. He catches it and smacks a third one out of the air.

"You want to set this entire kingdom on fire, all so you don't have to apologize to your sister? Are you that egotistical? You lot are so freaking dramatic. Not everything needs to come to some cosmic freaking battle. Sometimes we can do things the easy way!"

"Brohn, stop, stop!" Aarik dodges several pancakes, and takes a hit from one more. "Ok, ok! I will! I'll talk to her, geez."

The Weis loft is filled with the smell of cooked meat, bubbling gravy, fresh cooked bread, and laughter. Well, not the smell of laughter, the sound of laughter, the emotion of laughter. The ladies of the Penny Lich sit around their table talking about the last couple days. Ella talks about the look on the opponents' faces when she smashes her slugs into their guts. She then explains how the warping vest works.

Sycilia reenacts several of her smoother counters and attacks from the field, already wearing her uniform. She gleams with the early morning light.

Gwen feeds a bit of meat to Potsticker, who emerges from the oven.

There is excitement in the air as the women prepare for the final match of the tournament. Sycilia can see her brother's face when he loses, the final moment of proving that she has earned her place, that she is indeed better than him. That's when there is a knock at the door.

"I'll get it," Gwen says. She flows from the table to the door, her dress swaying in the light of the morning. "It's so fun having you both in such a good mood. It's terrible I know, but I hope to the Conclave that you smash Aarik's face in today."

"There ya go, girl!" Sycilia shouts.

"Just maybe not too much; it's such a pretty face," Gwen says.

"It's the same as my face, ya know," Sycilia wipes gravy from her mouth, smudging it on her cheek.

"But neither of us want to sleep with you, Sycilia," Ella says.

"That's unfortunate."

Gwen opens the door to see Aarik standing before her. "Pretty face! Er, I mean, Aarik!"

"Aarik?" Sycilia stands up and turns to the door.

"May I come in?" Aarik looks calm and somber. The cold morning light contrasts his face and shows growing shadows over his expression.

"Yes, of course," Gwen says.

"NO!" Sycilia shouts. "You stay right there."

"Well, she already said yes, so I'm just gonna–" He begins to take a step.

"Stop!" Sycilia shows her anger.

"Sycilia," Gwen hisses, "don't be rude."

"Me rude?!" She objects. "He rude!"

"I'm sure he's here for a very good reason," Gwen says, putting her hand on his shoulder, closing the door behind him.

"Gwen, don't fall for his li'l baby somber eyes. He did this all the time to our mom, and he got whatever he wanted. Now he's here to stir up trouble before the match, And I won't have it! I know you Aarik, and I know that you're just going to do something, like poison our food, so we have diarrhea on the field or something." She takes a goop of gravy on toast and shoves it in her mouth. "But I've already eaten, so you're too late!" Mock laughing at him she spits gravy all over the room.

"Unless he already snuck in and poisoned it," Ella says calmly, smelling some bacon, "and you just ate more of it." Sycilia twists to face Ella, eyes wide in fear. She then opens her mouth and lets all the food fall out on a plate.

"I didn't poison your food," Aarik says, stepping forward.

"Fat chance I believe you," Sycilia says. "I know you'll do anything to win, including giving your sister diarrhea in front of the royal court."

"Sis, I don't want you to diarrhea." He comes closer.

"Yeah, right. Just like you didn't want to leave for school, right? Just like you didn't leave me behind to fend for myself. Like you don't think you're smarter and better than me? Because you got chances that I was never going to be given? Yeah, right. You went to your diarrhea school and now you're back to give it to me! I bet you–"

"Damnit, Sycilia, I want to apologize!" Aarik shouts. The room goes quiet. Potstricker sneaks back into the oven. "Will you please stop talking about diarrhea for two seconds so I can say I'm sorry?"

Sycilia feels something new. It's not new, it's familiar, but it's different. She's felt embarrassment before, but this was odd. She was embarrassed for being right, for being the better person. And also for talking about poop so much. Her lips went white from being shut so tight.

"I'm sorry. Ok? I am. I'm the reason that we're in this mess. It's all my fault. And If I can fix it I will. But you need to understand something. I hope you can get through your anger and your pain, and I hope you can hear me when I say I never wanted to go to that damn school. I begged for dad to send you. Now that I've gone through it, after joining the fighters guild and having left, I'm glad I went. I would never want you to become a number like me."

"Pretentious like you," Sycilia says.

"Sure, I guess." Aarik tilts his head and agrees.

"Self-centered like you," Ella adds on.

"Hey now."

"Vapid, like you," Gwen adds.

"This is not a community forum, ok?" Aarik holds his hands up. "Sycilia, I was put through hell. I survived, always thinking about you and thinking about escape. So yeah, I come off strong because if I don't utilize everything I learned there, then the things I lost along the way, the sacrifices..." Aarik shakes his head, he sucks in air through his teeth and breathes deep, "everything I lost would be for nothing."

"I don't have a problem with who you are, Aarik," Sycilia says. She steps closer to him and moves her head to keep her eyes locked on his. "It's that you were given the opportunity, and I wasn't. It's that you think that who you became is what I should be, but I was held back."

"Sycilia," Aarik tries, but Sycilia holds her hand up.

"You don't get it. You sacrificed for what you have, but I have clawed and scraped for everything I have. I have fought tooth and nail for it all. And to see you go off, and come back, and... and, and I'm treated like a criminal just for being myself, while you get to be you and everyone celebrates it... I hate you for it." She said it. She had held onto it for years. She didn't even know she felt it, but she did. The well of anger was deeper than she knew. She sank into it. Hatred, hatred for men who had held her down. Her dad, Henderson Barker, her own brother. They all pushed her aside like she was nothing, and she despised the feeling. She began to shake in the realization. She gulped at the air, realizing she had not breathed in some time. Sycilia then refocused and saw her brother.

Tears welled up in his eyes, a sad sly smile cooked on his teeth. He was fighting the pain. She had hurt him. She had hurt him bad.

"It only seems right." He looks around, catching the faces of the others in the room. But they all appear as his father. All he sees is his dad, watching him. He nods, as the pain turns to anger. He sips on his lip, teeth latching to his cheek. "I was–" He tries to say it, he's never said it, never thought he'd have to, not with her. "I was exiled from my home, Sycilia. I was forced out of my home, not because I was honor bound, or because it was my duty."

Aarik looks at them all again.

"Dad caught me with one of the footmen," Aarik says, almost amused. "He caught me, and... and the next day he sent me away. I never had a chance to amend my actions, explain myself, or try to change his mind. He threw me out like trash because I didn't live up to his expectations of a Gentleman. I didn't choose to go, and father didn't choose me over you. He punished me, punished us both, for what he assumed was an offense to his honor."

Again, the room is quiet.

Sycilia feels the earth shake, the world shift, her brain change. Aarik was a victim of her father, same as her. All these years she held onto a hate for her own sibling, because he was chosen and she was nothing, yet he suffered as much as herself. But how, how could she forgive him. After years of hatred, or malice and bottled emotions, how can she be rid of it? Her next words surprised even her.

Sycilia looked down at the ground to her left side and jetted forward her jaw in irritation. "Which footman?"

Aarik is uncertain in his answer, wondering if there is a trap being laid. "Uh, Salzman."

"SAMUAL SALZMAN!?" She explodes. "You made out with Samual Salzman?"

"Uh, yeah?"

"He ended up losing his mind and killing the chef!"

"No!" Aarik says in shock. Sycilia moves toward him.

"They were lovers and Salzman found out that the chef was cheating on him. Lost his mind and carved him up and served him to the family for dinner that night."

"That's disgusting! And terrible! And so funny!" Aarik laughs.

"And to think he was cheating on the chef with you!" Sycilia laughs as well.

"Yeah! I guess dad might have actually saved me on that one."

"Hey, whoa now, don't go crazy there," Sycilia says with a smirk.

"Yeah, dad's still the worst."

"The worst, right?!" Sycilia eggs Aarik on.

"What was it like when Salzman brought the chef out for you all? Was it on a silver platter?"

"Oh my gosh, it was the craziest thing. We were sitting there waiting forever...."

Gwen walks over to Ella, both watching the siblings bond over the grisly death of a former servant. "Are they, uh? Are they making up?" Gwen asks.

"Seems like it," Ella says.

"So are we just gonna, like, not go to the tournament?" Gwen asks.

"Shhh," Ella puts her finger on Gwen's mouth. "I don't wanna miss out on what the chef tasted like."

The Valeward Scatterbattle arena is filled to the brim with onlookers. The royal houses fill their private patios and balconies. Even the Mistress watches, alone, from the Evergreen podium. Flags whip in the air, and the mountain lets loose white plumes of smoke. The cold crisp air smells of snow as clouds begin to form in the distance.

Sycilia and Aarik stand on the field and look out at the spectators.

"You're not gonna hit me as hard now that you don't hate me right?" Aarik asks.

"I dunno, I have quite a few years of pent up aggression toward the men in our family. And you do look a lot like our father."

"That's not my fault, plus you look like him too."

"Which is why I'm banning mirrors from the Weis loft after today."

"If you even get to live there. I still plan on living in the Crowder Tower. But I'll let you come stay in the guest room."

"Oh, is that how it's gonna be?"

"Yeah, I think it is. So, maybe just let me win and we both have a place to sleep tonight."

"I'm sure Ella will invite you up to her attic."

Aarik puts his hand on Sycilia's shoulder. "I'll

throw the game right now if you think there's a chance that could happen."

"Play your best, let's have some fun," Sycilia says as she smacks his head playfully. She winks and runs toward the gold buttress.

The crowd begins chanting and cheers as Aarik watches Sycilia find her place, he smiles and straps his armor down. "Finally time to prove once and for all who is better."

"I can't believe how fast we lost," Brohn says, helping Aarik to the door. They lean on each other, limping and covered in bandages. Aarik shouts out as he falls in front of Brohn's house. "I mean, she really let us have it. It was like trying to out maneuver an octopus. She was everywhere."

"Please, Brohn, stop talking. Your voice is hurting my groin."

"Yeah, she struck you right in the boys, eh? That's crazy, like she didn't even have to, she went out of her way to smack that beanbag and drop you."

"I know, I was there."

"I'm just saying, I thought we were at least gonna put up a better fight than that, maybe not win. But still, better than that."

"It wouldn't hurt so bad if Crowder didn't have all my stuff thrown out of the apartment before we got back to it."

"Yeah, he seems pretty pissed."

Aarik readjusts and grunts. "Well, I did let down the legacy of one of the prominent families in the city. So, you know, a normal weekday for me."

"Yeah." Brohn lingers on the front step with Aarik for a moment, then slaps his knee. "Well, I'll get a kettle on, and we can get an ice bath going for you. I'll even cook some flapjacks, just for you."

Aarik groans as he stands. Pain shoots through his body, but returns to one point. He grabs his crotch as he turns and supports his fragile...ego.

Immediately Aarik is hit with the smell of a thousand apples, the warmth of a hug from a bear, and the comfort of paradise. His eyes take in the lavish and open home. Warm tones of wood, soft pelts, and overstuffed cushions.

"You're welcome to stay here with me if you like," Brohn says. "If you don't mind it, I mean. I know how much you liked your tower. And this is more of a halfling hole--"

"This is beautiful." Aarik says. He breathes in the scent of a homecoming, a place to lay his head. He closes his eyes as he thinks back to his childhood home.

T.W. CLAWSON

Deathly Hallowed Grounds

Frost forms on the trees, melts, evaporates on the ground from the heat of the cold white sun, and then crystallizes quickly by the tree tops. Fog fills the air of the late evening road. Ella the hunter, dressed in a leather jacket, armed with daggers, swords, a cross-bow, and a whip, walks down the road of Valeward to the southeast part of town. ext to her is Sycilia, her best friend.

A vest made of metal chains shows off Sycilia's bulky dark-skinned arms, a massive black blade on her back.

On Ella's other side is Aarik, a lean and handsome man. He slightly resembles his twin sister, their hair the same–black to white–their eyes the same–brown. Sycilia is determined to prove herself, and Aarik is determined to get laid. Aarik keeps his bow in some unknown space, but his arrows sling on his right hip, the belts accentuating his frame. Ella bites her lip.

"Are you even listening to us, Ella?" Aarik says as he turns to see her staring at him. She looks away and he smiles.

"I wasn't, no."

"Gotta love how honest she is," Aarik says and he slides next to her and puts his arm around her shoulder."

"We were talking about how ridiculous Elliot is," Sycilia says.

"In what way?"

"Him refusing to join us for this job," Aarik says. "Total nerf move."

"It makes sense," Ella says. "He's a business owner now. He has to maintain the business."

"But we're his friends! We're a party of adventurers, and we need a healer."

"It seems like he's done the work of providing for us. We only have this job because he and Moses have to spend time getting us these jobs. Seems like he's being his normal honorable self."

"True," Sycilia says.

"Well, what the hell?!" Aarik shouts. "You're just gonna switch sides like that?"

"She's right though. He's being a good leader to us."

"I just wanna complain about our boss!" Aarik says. "And now you two are gonna defend him?! Just 'cause you didn't treat your underlings well as a crime boss, doesn't mean Elliot is a celestial. He still kicked us out of the tavern, remember!?"

"I was pretty good to my gang members, but still, the more I think about it, the more I'm realizing Elliot is really doing us a favor."

"You two are the worst."

"Hey!" A voice calls to them from behind. They turn to see a figure in the cold Gaze air.. The figure is running to them waving their hands.

"Who is that?" Sycilia asks.

"Elliot? Telling us to come back?" Aarik says.

"I doubt it," Ella says. "He's nerdy, but he's stubborn."

"There it is." Aarik laughs. "I want all those ex-wifely deets."

"Hey guys, hold up," the figure says in the fog.

"What kind of details would you like?"

"I don't know, what do you have? Something salacious."

"Well, I've seen him naked several times"

"Come on," Sycila says annoyed.

"Yeah, that's it." Aarik laughs again. "What's he packing? Are we talking goblin, orc or ogre?"

Sycilia punches Aarik. "That's enough." At that point the figure breaks through and Gwen appears.

"Gwen!" Aarik says. "What are you doing out here?"

"I came to–" She huffs and breathes deeply. "I came out here to join." She sticks her finger up and catches her breath. "I came to join you."

"You came to join our quest? Are you qualified to do that?" Ella asks.

Gwen sneers and responds impatiently, "Yes." She then thinks about it. "Well, no. But I am a part of the guild, technically. And I have to do some extra jobs to help pay rent now; can't expect my dad to take care of everything for me."

"So you're gonna come fight a monster just so you pay rent?" Syscilia asks.

"Isn't that what you guys do?"

"It's fine, she can join us." Aarik puts his arm around her shoulder. She blushes. "And then you all live happily ever after in your new cottage together, or die trying."

"I don't know," Ella says. "No offense, Gwen, but this can get very dangerous very quickly."

"It's ok, I brought these!" Gwen pulls out a rolled pouch and unstraps it. Inside the pouch are many pockets filled with glowing tubes.

"Is that bottled fired?" Aarik looks closely.

"Yep."

"How?"

"I spend a lot of time with Potsticker," Gwen says.

"Ew! You milked Potsticker?" Aarik backs up.

"In a way, I guess. Same way you milk a snake. Look, I promise to stay out of the way and provide help where I can. I also cooked up a couple elixirs to help with injuries and stuff." She pulls out another pouch with a few glowing bottles of ethereal liquid.

"When did you learn to make all this stuff?" Sycilia asks.

"I dunno, I talk to a few artificers often, and I've picked up stuff every once in a while."

"Then it's settled!" Aarik says. "She's a valued member of this guild, and she wants to pay her way in life as an adventurer. She gets an equal share in the spoils."

"Thank you, Aarik," Gwen says.

"Just be careful," Sycilia says, then turns to walk down the path. Ella looks her over for a moment, and watches as Aarik helps her put the potions away. When Ella turns to catch up to Sycilia, her hair flips out quickly and her eyes squint in irritation.

Aarik leads Gwen down the road. "Ok, so give us the deets on your dad. What is it about him that drives you crazy? Also, what's he working with down there: a goblin, orc or ogre?"

The D'qoury Estate:

A towering mansion the size of two Penny Liches joined together, the D'qoury estate is surrounded by a massive plot of land. A Farm, an orchard, and a great cemetery to the south of the wall. The sun reaches its zenith, but storm clouds encroach.

"Lady D'qoury," Sycilia says as she sips on a cup of tea, "Elliot says that you would like us to take care of something troubling you."

"Indeed," Lady D'qoury says, her brown hair loose

on her shoulders, and her proper robe pulled tight around her waist. She is young compared to most royal house aristocats, which Aarik noticed immediately.

“If you don’t mind me asking, why don’t you take this to the Magecore? Seems like something they or the militia would be able to handle.”

“To be honest,” Lady D’qoury says, adding a bit of food to her plate, “I don’t want to deal with the MMistress. She has begun to consolidate Magecore power and seems increasingly more zealous about her own priorities. I would rather we work with local talent with no agenda.”

“What agenda does the Mistress have?” Sycilia pushes.

“There’s more to her plays lately than I think you understand. She seems fanatic about something coming, and she has been doing everything she can to prepare for it. So I would rather not owe her something, not when I have my entire estate and my family’s legacy to protect.”

“What is it that vexes you, Lady D’qoury?” Ella pulls out her notebook.

Lady D’qoury breathes deep, then snaps her fingers. One of her manservants drops a box on the table between them all. It opens and inside is a head. The smell penetrates their noses and they gasp for air. Rotten flesh peels from the bone, and the eyes droop as they decay in their sockets. But what throws them off more than anything is that the head shivers and moves. Its jaw opens and closes and it wiggles, trying to free itself from the cloth inlay of the chest.

“Good Lords!” Aarik shouts. Gwen backs up and stifles a scream. Sycilia plugs her nose and squints trying to get a better look.

“Meet my uncle Morty,” Lady D’qoury says. “Uncle

Morty, meet the Penny Lich crew."

"Hey, how's it goin'?" The Morty head says.

"It talks?" Aarik says appalled.

"He does."

"I do."

"Why?"

Lady D'quory says, "There's something out in the cemetery that is digging up the dead and restoring a piece of life back to them."

"It's a freaking necromancer lady, or somethings," Morty rasps. "After I cames to, I saw it do it to a couple of my cousinses. And I'll tell you what, the world was already a sour enough place with thems alive onces. Conclave knows we don't needs another round of thems awfulnesseses...es."

"Hey, can we all acknowledge the undead thing's talking to us?" Gwen says.

"Seems reasonable enough," Ella says.

"No, she's right," Sycilia says, still covering her mouth and nose. "This is weird."

Lady D'qoury holds a napkin to her mouth and nose. "The effect is temporary, but it's still significant enough to cause damage to my property–and my reputation. Worse still, someone might get hurt or killed by one of these undead creatures."

"I personally think it's just irresponsible," Morty begins. "I mean, a second life with no's respect for the laws of nature. Look, I'm a fun lovin' guy, that's what I was known for in life, Fun Lovin' Mort, but hey, dead is dead. And whoevers this necro-chick is, she doesn't care much for the laws of--" Suddenly the head stops and a soft white puff of condensation rises from the mouth. The head is, once again, dead.

Lady D'qoury snaps her fingers again. "Pity." The man servant closes the lid and takes the chest out of the room. The group breathes in the fresh air deeply. Ella watches Lady D'qoury for a moment.

"Go into the cemetery and kill this creature. And don't get yourself killed, because then I have to clean it up," the Lady says.

"I'm just saying, if we start selling these at the bar, then we get some extra money, and everyone is happy," Moses says, holding up a burlap sack, filled with lumps and dripping some viscous goop.

"Moses," Elliot responds, pushing the lump sack away from his face. "We're not going to sell these in the bar. This is something of the Nightmare King. It smells awful."

"Come on, dude, they're a local business that needs a little marketing help," Moses says.

"And it seems like some recipe help, too," Brohn adds as he lumbers over, his large frame shadowing over the other two. "There's no way I'm gonna eat one of those."

"They're great," Moses begins taking one out of the sack. The stench of the lumps immediately fills the air around them, and Elliot and Brohn both choke on the scent.

Moses had guarded himself, but breathes out saying, "You guys are overreacting." He then makes the mistake of breathing in, and the toxic unrealmly stink fills his lungs. He coughs hard and slaps the bar. He then looks at the blackened, lumpy bar of "food." It's covered in mucus, with bits of solid food sticking out of it.

"Don't do it," Elliot says.

Moses watches the thing, giving it the same eye as any evil he's faced. He's determined.

"Seriously, Moses," Brohn says, "don't put that in your body."

It takes every part of divine strength Moses has to quickly shove the snack into his mouth.

"Ugh!" Brohn gags. Elliot grimaces while watching the paladin shove down the horrid food. His throat audibly forcing it back up, he focuses with all his might and pushes it back down. His stomach rejects the muck clump. Moses' face wrenches like something screws up his butt. He stares off into the middle distance, odd noises coming from his body. Within a few seconds he stops breathing and sits like a statue.

"Moses?" Elliot says, waving his hand in front of his friend's face. "Come on buddy, you ok?"

An unnerving growl escapes Moses' lips. Without him moving, he begins to let out the air left in his lungs. "Uuuuuuuuuuuuuuuh," he begins, then quickly snaps back to normal. "Uuuuualll good dude!"

Moses jumps up and claps.

Brohn steps back. "You gonna hurl?"

"Nah, bro. I feel great. Those are awesome."

Elliot puts his hand on Moses' shoulder. "You don't have to do this, bud."

"Do what? These are great. Hag Balls, that's what they're called, and man you can really taste the hag– and the balls." Moses tries to take a step, but stumbles.

"Moses," Elliot warns, "Don't."

"Don't what? I love it. I'm gonna say everyone in the guild has to eat one every morning. Great source of nutrition."

"I quit," Brohn says quickly. "Ain't no way I'm popping one of those balls in my mouth."

"Brohn, once you get past the salty, earthy...hulk."

"Moses," Elliot stands.

"No, no, I'm fine." Moses waves them off. "It just the after taste lingers; it's a sort of spicy oatmeal ling–

hulk." With the last lurch of his stomach, Moses lets his eyes glow in silver, and he stands upright. A light begins to fill the room, an aura around the paladin's body. For a moment he is an entity of celestial existence. His armor shimmers in silver and platinum, his hair flows with white. A form of pure light and goodness, he radiates peace and serenity. Then just as quickly as it starts, it ends. His armor goes back to bronze, and his eyes faintly glow of silver, his hair pulled back in long black strands.

"Did you just use divine intervention to digest that hag ball?"

"No." Moses says filled with guilt. "It was for the other poison in my body. I had to purify it, you know."

"There was a different poison?" Brohn asked. "What poison?"

"Uh, from an earlier quest I did. I just kinda forgot about it."

There's a knock on the door to the Penny Lich. The three of them look at the door quietly. The rapping happens again.

"Too early for the lunch crowd," Brohn says.

"Maybe a quest?" Moses says. He wipes his armor off, and answers the door. As soon as he opens it, his stomach lurches again.

A slender figure with a gaunt face, wearing black robes, stands looking down on Moses. Immediately the paladin recognizes the person.

"Grimander?" Moses walks outside into the cold white light, immediately feeling the chill snowy air. He closes the door behind him and keeps his eyes on the man.

"Moses, I hope that I'm not inconveniencing you."

"What do you need, Grimander?"

"I was hoping to speak to you and your business

partner about the offer I made you some time back."

"Look, now's not really a great time."

"Most of your staff is on a job, you have no patrons, Elliot is here, and so am I. What makes this a bad time?"

"Well, if you must know, I uh...have a cold. Yeah, I'm sick," Moses says, then sneezes a few times.

"Then why are you answering the door?" The Archfey asks, feeling slightly out of place standing in the street of the material plane.

"'Cause Elliot is worse off than me. So you know, not doing great at the moment."

"You haven't told him about the offer, have you?"

"Well, to be honest, no, I haven't."

"That's inconvenient. Things are starting to happen, Paladin Moses, and I would very much like to have you as an ally."

"Stop pressuring me."

"I'm not pressuring you, I just want--"

"Showing up at my door, forcing me to talk to you out in the cold below all the Hallowed Conclave, getting me sick." Achoo, Achoo, Achoo! "You think that's not pressure!?

"I didn't get you sick."

"Stop gaslighting me!"

Grimander cocks his right eyebrow.

"Good day sir!" Moses shouts as he begins to head inside.

"Moses, I really wish to help you and you–"

"I said good day!" The door slams and Grimander is left standing alone at the door to the Penny Lich.

"What was that about?" Elliot asks, throwing the hag balls in the fire.

"Just a pushy salesman."

"What was he selling?"

"Uh, he was selling, uh, Gnome Coffee."
"Gnome Coffee?"
"Yeah, freaking Gnome Coffee, coffee made with real gnomes."
"You mean by, right?" Elliot asks.
"No, I mean with, Elliot, " Moses says indignantly. "Are you going to make me repeat everything?"
"No, I just.... I'm sorry man."
Knock Knock. The three of them look at the door again.
Knock Knock.
"I'll get it," Elliot says.
"No!" Moses says running over to the door again. "I got it."
Brohn and Elliot exchange an odd look.
"Probably just the coffee guy, again." Moses says, inching to the door. He grabs it and spins as he flings it open. "Like I said before, scram!"
As soon as the light hits his eyes and he sees who stands at the doorway, his stomach lurches again.
A young woman and a small boy stand in the whipping snow.
"Sir, I would like to employ you to watch my son," the woman says.

The cemetery on the southeastern border of Valeward is something like a city for the dead. Mausoleums tower above the the foggy air, dripping with defrosting dew. The ivory and marble structures are adorned with winged creatures and reaper-like figures, guardians protecting the resting and sentries watching for the wandering living soul. Those that have yet to give up the ghost walk feel the uneasy stare of death around every corner.

Sycilia says, "I've spent plenty of time in the cemeteries of my home town, and this is so much more."

Ella says, as she leads the party, "While, this is technically a necropolis, this is quite small compared to some of the cemeteries I've hunted in. King City, for instance. The whole town was originally a necropolis for Valeward royalty–a place to rest and look out at the Yonder Valley Lake."

"You're lore dumping again," Sycilia says.

"Shh," Aarik presses. "What happened to the graves there?"

"They were mostly moved into the gorges and caves of the mountains around the city. The Guardian that used to rest within the mountain tore out of there a few hundred years back and left a massive opening in Mount Jib."

"A Guardian?" Gwen asks.

Aarik jumps on the question. "It was a massive mechanical sentry that roamed the valley. Last time it was seen, it was acting as a bridge on the Babbling Bard River in Haberdashery Woods. I didn't realize it had been in King City before that."

"That's what they say at least," Sycilia says. "But, honestly, I'm not too concerned about all that. I want to find this nercro-lady and bring her head to Lady D'qoury." Sycilia pulls her blade out. The black metal gleams in the light of the descending sun. It cuts through the thick fog and collects chilling dew.

Gwen, pulling a couple bottles of liquid fire out, shakes slightly, letting the glass clang as she prepares. Aarik looks at her and smiles. She gives him a weak smile and stands straight. Confidence courses through her, and as he winks at her, she feels every bit of fear leave her body.

Aarik holds his hand out and a quick snap of light

brings forth his bow. Dark wood wrapped in leather and tasseled with a couple odd charms on the ends. He knocks an arrow and squints his right eye to peer through the fog.

Ella holds up her hand crossbow and points to the two pathways before them, “Time to split up, I think.”

“I think you’re right,” Sycilia nods at Ella and the two ladies diverge into separate swaths of mist.

“She’ll take good care of you.” Aarik doesn’t look at Gwen, but his words are directed toward her. “Make sure you do the same for her.”

“I will be sure to help her stay in one piece.” Gwen smirks.

Gwen walks through the cemetery, holding the bottled fire in both hands. She can feel warmth. This place was dreary and cold; the bottles were a nice change, and she was craving it. Fire never seemed to bother her as much as it did others, though she can still feel burns and pain from natural fires. This fire though, the fire of an Elemental, is something special; it is a part of her, the way water is a part of the human body. Like oxygen is a part of the blood. Like shit is a part of the earth, and fertilizer and food are a part of the cycle.

“Gross,” Gwen says as she realizes they use food waste to help grow food.

“You can say that again,” Sycilia says from beyond sight.

Gwen breaks through the obscured field. As she does, she sees what Sycilia is talking about. A patch of land riddled with headstones, some old, some ancient, warped by time, crooked and facing in every direction–an acre of toothy rows surrounded by statues and mausoleums.

Brown grass, with frosted tips, rips through the cold,

hard ground. The yard of death would be enough to make the skin crawl in its own right. An alley way of rot and decay. Solace and quiet, this place speaks loudest in whispers of the past.

But then, as the rolling fog clears, the reveal comes like the stench of the dead. Tombstones stand over holes in the earth where bodies had laid in peace, now showing their departure.

Gwen shakes as she takes in the sight. "Sycilia?"

"You got those bottles ready?"

"Yes."

"Good." Sycilia walks through the yard of death, keeping her sword ready for attack.

"Is...is this worth the paycheck?" Gwen hisses.

"Already having second thoughts?" Sycilia smirks. "We haven't even seen anything."

"I saw a talking head earlier. I think that counts as 'something.'"

"A little necromancy and you're out the door, eh?"

"Can you stop pretending like this is normal?"

'What can I say, Gwen? You're a part of a guild led by the divinely chosen. You're a companion with a Hunter and a Spellsword. And all this is after you got back from battling a magic being in the long forgotten temple of this land's Dragon King. And you're concerned about a little dark magic?"

"You know, the more you talk, the less I find myself comfortable with living in this world."

"I'll keep you safe, I promise."

"That's not my concern. I know I can take care of myself." Gwen walks ahead a little and peers through the mist. She then turns and looks back at Sycilia, "We're doing this for...what? Why would people live a life that puts them in danger so much? We jumped so quickly into a quest we didn't really assess what we were doing."

"This is how life goes for some people. They choose to solve problems in unorthodox ways. The solution to the problem isn't what they're after–it's the journey provided by the problem."

"And you're one of those people?"

"Yeah." Syscilia swings her sword and walks around a corner to find a new yard of open graves. She looks down and sees a coffin with a broken lid.

Gwen joins her in looking down at the dark hole. "Why?" Sycilia stays quiet for a moment. She then lowers down to her knees and looks at the ground around the grave. She picks up some of the dirt and watches as it slips from her fingers. "What do you see?" Gwen asks, getting close to the falling dirt.

"Nothing," Sycilia says. "I'm just avoiding the question."

"What? Why?"

"I dunno, man," Sycilia says, exhausted. "'Cause I don't like talking about myself."

"Why?"

Sycilia shoots annoyance toward Gwen, who smirks back at her.

"You ever heard of the Rummagers?"

"No."

"For the last couple hundred years, Valley Gate has had a thriving criminal underground. They also have a thriving militia presence, do you know much about Valley Gate?"

"River traffic, timber, and ships pass through–very important to the Kingdom, yep."

"Ok, cool, just trying to set up the scene here."

Gwen continues, "In the northwest corner of the valley, a city built on two hills looks down upon a river, where the two factions of good and evil are in constant strugg–"

"Ok, I get it," Sycilia says. "Whatever, anyway,"

"Centuries ago, the city was torn apart by the attack of flying ships and mechanized monsters. Valley Gate holds not only the door to the Babbling Bard River, but the story we find our heroes in...."

Sycilia holds her blade up. "Seriously, enough."

"Sorry, I read a lot of the Olenor Accounts as a kid." Gwen looks at the sword and closes her mouth.

Sycilia drops the blade and explains, "Our father wanted me to marry an officer, even sent me to work with the militia so I could get close to him. When I realized I didn't want the same thing, I joined the Rummagers: a gang that ran the south west side of town. They were actually contracted by the kingdom to go through the old southern ruins and find relics and such. I joined their searches and enjoyed it. But uh, ya know, they were a gang, and gangs fight over territory, same as governments. I got really good at defending what was ours, and I ended up becoming a warlord of sorts."

"A warlord? That sounds impressive." Gwen giggles a little.

"It was a big deal." Sycilia stabs the ground with her blade. "I had to kill a lot of people to get there. I left my family, my position, I gave up on most of my morals. I lived like a queen."

"Sounds like you miss it."

"No." Sycilia snaps back from the memories of her old life. "Not really. I was high on the ego of it all. And then it all came tumbling down. And I was taken into custody, shown the consequences of my actions, and I begged to make it right. I was given two options and I chose the one that brought me to Valeward."

The girls walk for a bit longer in silence. The cold air

of Gaze month had settled in; snow accumulated on the ridgelines and fences. The sky was dark, threatening more snow at any point, and only the hardiest of birds flew about digging for worms and rodents.

"This life," Sycilia begins again, "the way we do things, who we are as a guild, I chose it." They come to a crossroads in the low hanging fog. The cobblestone path split into several directions and led into the unseen.

"Everytime I come to a crossroads, I make the choice; I never let others choose for me. That's what this life is about. It's about the freedom to make your own choices. If you want to do things the mundane way, then by all means go back on the path you came on. Let Elliot tell you what drinks and food to make. Go back to living with your father. Let them choose who you will marry." Sycilia turns to the other pathways "But if you want to join adventures and make your own choices, then choose a new path. And be ready to fight for that life every step of the way."

"Which one?" Gwen looks at the three directions in front of her. The fourth is the path back, and in a split second she knows she would never take it.

Sycilia smiles. "It doesn't matter. The moment you start moving is the moment the Conclave can direct you. As long as you're moving forward, then you can't make a wrong choice."

Gwen smiles at the advice. She lifts her head and breathes in deep. Her lungs fill with the cold evening air. Long shadows cast from the late hour blend with the dreaded surroundings.

Gwen takes a step forward and makes her choice on a pathway. Her foot plants and she reconsiders for a moment, then, as she turns back to Sycilia, the woman winks at her and waves her sword like a wand. Gwen nods and turns back to her chosen direction, then walks forward.

The shadows of the statues linger. The buildings loom over her and the growling of the graveyard catches up to her. She pauses: growling?

"What's up?" Sycilia asks as she catches up.

"Do you hear that?"

"What?"

They look around and then see the shadows of the sculptures begin to move. Ahead of them, several silhouettes shamble toward them, hands out and voices caught in a groan. The figures begin breaking through the fog, rotten and decayed. Undead creatures come back from the grave, several of them stumble from Gwen's chosen path.

"Hey Gwen?" Sycilia readies her blade.

"Yeah?" Gwen responds in a black stare.

"You chose the wrong path."

The Hunter and Spellsword, Ella and Aarik creep through the dense fog with their weapons ready. A wooden arrow knocks on a string, pointing at the ground while Aarik keeps it tight and takes in the surroundings. The blue in the air is eerie as the sun sits at the lowest part of the horizon.

"The sunset in the northern sky is always the weirdest to me." Aarik takes in the sunset through the fog and clouds.

"It's my favorite month of the year," Ella says. "The sky grows silver instead of orange at sunset. It reminds me of the silver I use against a lot of anithropes and vampires."

"And demons?"

"No, demons horde silver and gold. It's iron that casts them out from the body. Them and Fey." Ella stops for a second and shivers and smiles. "Isn't this great, we're hunting the undead in a cemetery. This is what it's all about, ya know?"

"I guess?" Aarik smirks. He watches as she pushes her hair back around her ear. The fiery red pulls attention in the silver light.

"I enjoyed taking Olive to the academy, but it was so boring. No death, no excitement, no hunting."

"You really like this, huh?"

"I love it."

"Why do you love it so much? Is it all revenge for your father?"

"Conclave, no." She continues walking, and makes an exasperated face without acknowledging Aarik. "He knew what he was doing. His whole life was about taking down the Shadow Society. That would be like a child getting revenge on the ocean for a sailor dying at sea."

"He was destined to die at the hands of monsters?"

"It was a high probability. That's how it goes. I won't be mad about it; it's just math."

"You don't feel like they won and took something you love?"

"They did what's in their nature, and we do what's in ours. This isn't a game; they didn't win. He hunted until he couldn't anymore, then he tried again and it cost him his life. Now I'm here, and I will find them, and I will kill them all."

"But why?" Aarik takes her hand and looks her in the eyes. She tries to hold contact but her eyes shift back and forth. Then drop. "You seemed callous, but when we first met you were hurting and you were desperate."

"I do this...I love doing this because it was all I was taught as a child. The only place I have in this society is to be the hunter. Without that, I'm just an outcast. My father taught me how to function, and so I function. I love doing this because for every odd look and misunderstood emotion, every common phrase or intention that flies over my head, when I hunt I'm reminded that they still need me. I'm important." A screech pulses through the air. The two look in the direction and move quickly.

They make their way past a massive mausoleum, two stories tall and surrounded by gargoyles and wraiths made of stone. Aarik moves around with his bow out to his side. Ella silently runs, holding her crossbow to her chest. They slink like shadows through the graves and carvings. Around the building is a great and dead tree, reaching with empty branches into the white sky.

"So, why are you so much less determined to get yourself killed as a hunter nowadays?" Aarik asks as they come to the base of the tree. Ella keeps her eyes on the sky, breathing slightly heavier.

"Ella?"

"I think I like you," Ella says without looking at him. Aarik's eyes widen and he shakes his head in awe, a cracking smile opening wide. After a moment of silence, Ella darts her eyes down, back to the sky, then looks at Aarik.

"Did...did you hear what I said?"

"I did. I did? Yeah, I did." Aarik tries saying the same thing several times to try out several tones.

"You're making fun of me," Ella says, lowering her weapon to the ground. She blushes and begins to walk into the fog. Aarik jumps forward and cuts her off. His lean frame is larger than hers. She sees several ways to get around him, but lets him stop her.

"I'm not, I promise you, Ella. I'm not. I just, I don't know, I–"

"You're not interested in a weirdo like me," Ella says, trying to help him find the words.

"I'm not used to someone being so direct," Aarik says. "I'm used to games, and flattery, and flirting. You know, like pick up lines." He laughs. "Damn girl, can I use you to fight a troll, cause you're hot enough to activate their fire vulnerability."

Ella looks Aarik in the eyes, almost pleading. A goofy smile overtakes her face, and she chuckles an odd and distinct laugh. "That's awful."

Aarik laughs with her. "Yeah, I know. But it's one of my best lines."

"I mean, It's also very good. As trolls are known to have an aversion to fire. It's actually a genius premise, as far as terrible pick up lines go. But no person is hot enough, literally or metaphorically to ward off a troll. It would end in tragedy. You know that right?"

"Haha, yes, of course I do. The joke is supposed to be ridiculous so the person talks to me some more. But it's always a game of half truths and masks. But with you, it's straight to the point. I'm not used to that, you know?"

"No, not really. I know that feelings are weird, and I experience them differently than most, but I usually try to keep things as simple as I can. And I'm telling the truth; after you and I hunted that wizard werewolf, I started to see something in you that I haven't really seen in anyone else."

"Rugged good looks and a massive di–"

"A passion for helping people."

"Oh, yeah, that too."

Ella moves closer, putting her hand on his arm. Aarik moves in on instinct, his hand caressing her cheek, moving her red hair around her ear. He smiles as she looks away. His finger brings her chin up, and she reconnects to his gaze. The silver setting sun defused in the foggy air, reflects off her eyes, and she looks back and forth between his.

"I feel like I'm going to...." She starts, but catches her breath.

"Yeah? Gonna what?" Aarik teases.

"Like, I want to...."

"Want to what?"

She closes her eyes and leans in. "Like I want to kiss you." Aarik closes his eyes and begins to move for the kiss. Closing the distance between them, the silver sun silhouettes their shapes, the mist whips about them, and the wind slows.

Just as they're about to touch lips, a raspy, decayed voice breaks the moment. "Elderberry Monroe? Is that you?" The two stop their advance and look toward the tree to see the figure of an undead man standing before them, one eye socket empty, and an arm completely ravaged by rot.

The young woman and her son sit at a table in the Penny Lich. Elliot and Moses sit across from them. A roaring fire melts cold from the tips of their noses and cheeks.

"Ma'am, I have to say, this isn't something we generally offer as one of our services," Moses says, as Brohn brings the two guests a couple of mugs filled with warm drinks.

"I understand that, but this really is an extreme situation and I have no one else to turn to," the woman says. "See, my husband was in the Magecore, died in an encounter with a wild mage, and now I'm left a widow. But I have a chance to earn a way to North Calastem, to Drake Wall, where my family is from. If

I can get my son, Maxius, back there then I feel I can properly start over. But I need to get everything ready for the trip, and I can't do that while watching him."

"We're not babysitter's ma'am," Moses says. "We're a guild of fighters and such."

"I heard you were a guild for the people. Everyone says you help people that no one else will."

"You heard that about us?" Moses asks. "Yes! Word of mouth marketing is working."

"Well," Elliot interjects, "it's landed us a babysitting job."

"I can pay," the woman says quickly. "If that's what your reservation is. I have coin from Heresse's death. I just need a few hours to get our stuff packed and help the caravan ready itself."

"It's not about the coin, it's just...." Moses looks at Elliot, who waits for him to finish. He then looks at Brohn.

"She is a people," Brohn says, head tilted. "Her son is one too."

"I think we should help her," Elliot says.

"Thank you," the mother says as her son finishes his food. "I promise to be back as soon as possible and then never haunt your doorstep again." She plucks several gold coins out of her purse.

"Please, keep it for now," Elliot says. "Get what you must for the journey. Crossing the eastern mountains in Gaze will be a dreaded undertaking. We will collect at the end of the shift."

"And take this with you," Brohn says, handing the woman a flask of cooked broth. "Be sure to stay warm out there. May the Conclave look down on you with favor."

"You are too kind," the woman says as she gets up and makes her way out of the tavern. Moses and Maxius stare at each other.

"No need to thank us. See you soon," Elliot says, walking her out. Brohn waves at her as she blows a kiss to her son and closes the door.

"Great, well, you enjoy that one," Brohn says, dropping his smile and wiping down the bar top.

"What?" Moses looks over at the large framed man.

"Yeah, looks like you have your work cut out for you," Elliot says as he claps Moses on the shoulder.

"What!? No. Nooooo." Moses jumps up. "You two don't get to just drop this kid on me. I didn't even want this job. You two were the ones pushing for it."

Brohn heads to the back. "Hey, I was just following Elliot's lead, but I'm gonna be busy serving the lunch crowd. I won't have time for this little guy."

"Elliot, you were the one that took the job. This is on you," Moses says.

"Sorry bud, I have all this paperwork to fill out–you know, the stuff you refused to do while I was gone? I'm still catching up on it. Plus I gotta start planning the semperlunas party."

"What, are you two kidding me? I didn't even want this!" Moses shouts as Elliot and Brohn leave the room. "You can't just do this to a guy. I had plans too, you know. I was gonna do some polishing or something." Moses is defeated. He looks down at the boy sitting at the table.

"I ate a whole wheel of cheese and haven't pooped in three days," the boy says.

Moses stares at him.

The boy stares back.

"Yeah, me too, bud. Me too."

"Gwen, come on!" Sycilia pulls her partner backward

into the fog.

"Do you want me to throw a fire bomb?" Gwen says, holding the vial up.

"NO!" Sycila shouts.

"What, why?"

An undead creature throws himself out of the fog toward them, and Sycilia slashes at him with her blade. The slice takes his head clean off. The body falls down limp, but the head remains alive, growling and chomping.

"That's why," Sycilia says as she kicks the head. It flies into the nothingness, howling away. Sycilia grabs Gwen's shirt, focusing on her as she runs forward. "These things are alive, I don't know why, I'm not qualified to know, but they don't die unless the spell wears off. If you throw a firebomb at them, what's gonna happen?"

"They blow up." Gwen pulls out of Sycilia's grasp, and Sycilia releases her.

"They catch on fire. Then what?"

"They burn to death."

"They're already dead."

"They burn to second death. They burn to death again. They again, secondly burn to twice death?"

"They walk around, and they're on fire. Setting this whole place on fire. The bombs won't stop them."

"Oh, right. Yeah, I guess that makes sense," Gwen says, now keeping up with Sycilia as they make their way back.

"That 's the thing about me, Gwen. I may not be book smart like Elliot and Aarik, but I have street smarts. I look at the world and see things that others just miss. I use my head along with my brai--" A sudden scream and Gwen realizes that she's no longer looking at Sycilia. A short scream and Gwen is alone.

The girl looks around, but realizes the fog is too thick. “Syl? Syl?! Sycilia!?” She feels the fire in her blood flame up, and her hands begin to burn. Licking flames reach out and burn in the fog.

“SYL!”

“Down here! UGH. That smarts. Dern it to Heck!” Sycilia’s voice comes from below. Gwen scrunches her face and pushes her eyes to see past the fog. Her torch like hands waving in front of her, and the fog dissipates, revealing an empty grave. Well, mostly empty. It still has a broken coffin, dirt, and a young fighter who recently fell in to it.

“Sycilia, what are you doing?”

“I’m just taking a short rest, you know, stocking up on hit points and doing a little downtime activity. What does it look like? I was too busy paying attention to you, and I fell into this Conclave forsaken hole.”

“Well, get out, the undead are still coming, I can hear them,” Gwen says, keeping her fire hands away from Sycilia’s view, and looking out at the cemetery. Sycilia begins her ascent, digging her hands into the mud and pulling. As soon as her weight leans on the walls of the grave, the mud caves in on itself, and she slips back down to the bottom, covered in mud.

“Sycilia, come on, we need to go.”

“I’m just having the time of my life down here, honey bun, so why don’t you just leave me here?” “You want me to abandon you?” Gwen puts out her hands and twists to glare at Sycilia. Sycilia’s face tells a tale. Mostly one of annoyance.

“No, Gwen. I’m stuck. I need help.”

“I have health potions and fire bombs....”

“You’re useless.”

"Ella, is that you?" the zombie says.

"Uh," Ella croaks as she distances herself from Aarik.

"Stand back, Ella!" Aarik summons his bow and aims at the undead.

"Please don't do that," the zombie says, putting a hand up. An arrow flies into it, piercing through so that the head breaches the back of the hand. A second one flies quickly and lands in the creature's chest.

"There's more where that came from, fiend!"

"This is who you're dating now? Some try hard merc?" the zombie asks, taking a casual stance.

"Do I know you?" Ella asks, putting her hand on Aarik's arm, stopping him from shooting again.

"Seriously? Ella, it's me," the zombie says, gesturing to himself. He points at his face with the hand that has an arrow in it. "It's Xander. Xander Grishwell?" Ella's eyes pop open in surprise. She leans in and takes a closer look at the dead man. Xander strikes a pose and moves his hands with pazazz, though his dead arm has a hard time responding.

"Oh my goodness. Xander?"

"In the flesh," He says, taking the top of his head off the skull and tipping it at her. "At least what's left of it."

"Oh my Deities, how are you?" A nervous and excited tone emanates from Ella's voice.

"I'm good, I'm good. Well, you know, sleeping for all eternity. Though I seem to be resting less than a corpse normally does, ammai right?"

"I'm sorry," Aarik says, lowering his guard and looking very confused. "What's going on here? Who is this?"

"This is Xander," Ella says matter of factly.

"Yeah, man, I just introduced myself," Xander says.

"Did you see my head flesh trick?"

"Ok, fine, but WHO is he?"

"He's Xander." Ella says, slightly annoyed. Xander agrees, matching her tone

"Seriously, my name is Xander, buddy."

"OK, hold on." Aarik thinks through his next words as he looks between them. "Why is Xander on a first name basis with you? Why isn't he trying to eat our flesh, and why does he seem to be needlessly aggressive toward me?"

"Oh, ok," Ella says. "I understand now. Yeah, Xander is my ex-boyfriend."

"We dated," Xander agrees.

"You, you dated?"

"He hard of hearing?"

"No, I'm not hard of hearing. I'm just confused. You dated this guy, and then what? He died and you buried him out here?"

Ella and Xander smile, exchange a look, and laugh.

"I don't like being out of the loop." Aarik says.

"Whoa, whoa, buddy," Xander says. "I'm sorry. We'll catch you up."

"I started dating Xander a few years back when I was looking for information on the Shadow Society. I had heard that they were using this place to hide bodies. I dug some up and started interviewing them."

"You did what? Wait, you interview them? The dead bodies? You interviewed the dead bodies?"

"Yeah...."

"They were dead, and you exhumed them, and then talked to them?"

"Yeah."

"Just like you're doing now, bud," Xander says. Ella walks up to Xander, picking a bit of muck off his tattered clothing.

"When I came across Xander here, he answered my questions, but there was just something about him I liked."

"It wasn't my mug, I can tell you that. It's definitely my personality."

"We kinda hit it off, and I decided to come back the next night, and the night after that, and soon it became a standing reservation."

"Candlelit dinners, moonlit walks, your basic low light activities." Xander raises what used to be his eyebrows.

"You dated...a zombie. He was dead, you brought him back to life, and then you went on dates and stuff."

"Yeah, that's what I just said."

"And then you, uh. I mean." Aarik's stomach lurches, and he keeps himself from gagging, eyes watering. "You uh, consummated the relationship?"

"What?" Ella looks stunned.

"You know–" Aarik smashes his hands together a few times. "--committed necrophilia..."

"Oh! Gross!" Xander says.

"No!" Ella squirms.

Aarik relaxes and feels the tension in his stomach drop. "Oh, thank the Deities."

"Make sure you get the joints."

Moses sits on one of the comfy leather chairs in front of the fireplace. He works on polishing his armor, getting deep into the fingers of his gauntlets. At his feet is the young boy who uses a rag to work on the feet of Moses' armor. Moses looks up at one point and hisses, "No, Maxius, no!" The boy stops and looks up. "You need to do counter clockwise circles." Moses shows him with the gauntlet and rag.

"Ok, Mister Mosley,"
"Moses."
"You know that cake is made with flowers?"
"Mhmm, just focus on the task at hand, buddy."
"Well, look at that," Elliot says coming out of his office. The tavern is filled with the usual midday guests, and Elliot wades through them. "Looks like someone's got a handle on this babysitting thing after all."
"Yeah, it's great. I promise him cake and he'll do literally anything."
"Mister Mosley says he's gonna give me a cake in the shape of a pony, and I can ride it while I eat it."
Elliot nods and smiles at the boy, then turns and scowls at Moses. "What is wrong with you?"
"What?"
"You can't keep promising him cake."
"Sure I can," Moses says. He drops his sword by Maxius. "Hey bud, if you shine this up for me, I'll make you a cake in the shape of your mama. How's that sound?"
"Really, Mister Mosley?"
"Hellsrealm, yeah! Cake for everyone." Moses turns back to Elliot. "See, just did it. He's happy, I'm happy, everyone is happy."
'First of all," Elliot says, "you shouldn't let him near your blade. That's dangerous; he's like six."
"He's seven and fifteen quarters."
"That's not a number, and exactly, too young to be handling your sword, you moron. And you can't keep promising him a cake he's never gonna get–that's lying. Don't you paladins have a code against lying?"
"That's lying to people. Children aren't people."
"Yes they are!" Elliot shouts. "Didn't you save a girl from death while I was gone? what happened to that guy?"

"She was a witch, and that was more Ella's thing than mine. Also, she was ten, not seven."

"And thirty seven fifteenths," Maxius adds in.

"See?" Mosese says.

"See? See what?" Elliot demands. "What he says doesn't prove any point you made."

Moses stands up and puts his hands on Elliot's shoulders. "Chill dude. I got this. He's fine. And besides, you put me in charge. So you need to let me do it. I'm obviously crushing it and probably one of the best babysitters in the city. So go back to your precious paperwork."

"This is a fine blade, Paladin Moses." A young voice says with the diction of aged experience. Elliot and Moses both look down at Maxius.

He holds the blade in his hands the way a warrior would–with respect and awe. "It must belong to the Summerhill lineage and represent much honor for your family," the boy of seven and sixty four thirds says. His eyes cover in a fog and his hair floats, bits of glitter and stars floating within it.

"I've been trying to reach you concerning the extension of work from my estate to your guild," the boy says.

The mud is caked on Sycilia's arms as she tries for the umpteenth time to climb out of the grave.

"I really hate to bother you, but if you don't hurry up, I'm gonna have to fight some zombies by myself," Gwen says.

"Will you please get a rope or something?"

"We're in a graveyard, Syl." Gwen looks around, trying to figure out where she can get something helpful. "Where am I supposed to get a rope?"

"As an adventurer, you should always have fifty feet of rope on you. It's the most important tool in your pack," Sycilia says.

Gwen looks down with irritation, blood boiling with anger, which is different from boiling with the fire of dragon kind. "Oh, great. Go ahead and throw yours up and I'll tie it off."

Sycilia looks up. Silence passes. Sycilia's bottom lip squishes between her teeth.

"You didn't bring it did you?"

"We're in a graveyard!" Sycilia shouts, "Why would I need one?"

"Oh, I don't know, maybe in case you fall in a grave!"

"That was never part of the plan!"

"And fighting zombies was?" A groan of undead rattles from the mist. Gwen pops her head up and sees the figure coming. The thing shambles forward, it's dead eyes locked on Gwen. The girl looks around for something. She flicks her hands and they catch fire. The creature comes closer. She throws a bolt of fire at its shoulder. The flesh catches, but the figure is unphased.

"You were right," Gwen shouts out.

"About what?"

"Fire."

"You didn't."

"I did."

"How many are there? Are they completely consumed?"

"One and only his shoulder. He doesn't look happy."

The rotting corpse stares the girl down as it stumbles across the ground with blackened and shrunken feet. His fingernails are still as long as when he died, but sharpened by the scratching and shoveling it took to escape the grave.

"Lead it to me," Sycilia's says from the grave.

"What?"

"Lead it to me, and then I'll take care of it down here."

"You wanna fight a zombie in a grave?"

"No," Sycilia says annoyed. "But you can't take these things on, I can. I can at the very least cut it to ribbons so it won't bother anyone. And I don't need you questioning me, just listen and we can get through this. I am here to keep you safe and this is what I need to d–" A body thumps on the coffin in front of Sycilia. Its shoulder is on fire, its bones broken and decayed. Sycilia quickly places her blade in the head of the creature. The writhing mass before her stops, sinking into the broken coffin below.

"Did it work?" Gwen peeks over.

"Yea." Sycilia breathes heavy. "Next time, a little heads up."

"So needy."

"What are you doing out here?" Xander asks as he and Ella walk through the cemetery together. Aarik follows behind. His bow at the ready.

"We're actually on a job," Ella says, taking the arrow out of Xander's hand. "The Lady D'qoury hired us to look into the recent rising of dead in her graveyard."

"So what was a typical date like?" Aarik barges in. "Drinks and smooching? Or were you two just hot and heavy from the beginning?"

"Aarik, relax," Ella says. "We mostly just talked about our lives, and family, and stuff."

"Oh, like all the stuff you and I talk about?" Aarik gesticulates in anger. "You're saying I'm the same as a dead guy?"

"Hey! Just cause I'm dead don't mean I'm unfeeling."

Aarik stares as Xander for a moment, rage seething below a calm face, then it explodes. "You eat people's faces!" He turns to Ella. "Does Elliot know about this?"

"Who's Elliot?"

"He's my ex," Ella says.

"Another boyfriend?" Xander chuckles and puts his elbow into her arm.

"Actually," Aarik says, "he's an ex-husabnd, and he's a cleric. And my boss. So, you know, you better watch out."

"You married the priest? My plan worked?" Xander smiles.

"Mostly, I mean, yeah. We got the demon, but there were other complications."

"Wait a minute, you getting married was his idea?"

"Well, we came up with it together over dinner," Ella says.

"You dated this guy, then you married a cleric, and now you're now you're–I'm at a loss for words."

"You said you're looking into the source of all this dead rising thing, right?" Xander asks.

"Yea," Ella continues to watch Aarik, unsure of how he feels about the situation.

"Well, I'd be happy to take you to her, if you'd like."

Aarik and Ella both turn to him.

"You know her?" Aarik asks.

"Sure, how do you think I came back to life again?"

"What is she? A harpy? A hagraven? A necromancer? A–"

"Ella, I can just show you," Xander says with a smile.

"He's working for her." Aarik jumps forward. "He's working for her, and he's going to try and get us killed."

"How?" Ella asks.

"He'll betray us, or something...."

"He's already admitted he works for her."

"Yeah, mate, I already said that."

"And he's already said he's gonna take us to her."

"I'm already doing it."

"But he's a zombie, and you...you kissed him. And you were about to kiss me. And now he's gonna take us to the evil lady." Aarik slumps down on a grave stone and stares off into the distance.

"Hey Xander, could I have a minute with him alone?"

"Oh, sure. Anything for you babe."

"Thanks." Ella squeezes his arm and turns to Aarik. Xander shuffles off into the fog. After taking a moment to watch Aarik, Ella slides down a grave next to him.

"I'm not good at this, ya know," Ella says.

Aarik chuckles. "Seems like you're a little too good at this."

"What does that mean?"

Aarik turns to face her. "You were dating a guy that could only exist when you wanted him to. You had complete control over the relationship. Then you went and married Elliot. You tricked him into falling in love with you. And it worked because you maintained control of the relationship. And now, you let me in a little bit more, but only when you want. It's obvious how I feel about you, but up until an hour ago, I figured I was a mild form of entertainment for you. You keep everyone at a distance, so you can maintain control."

Ella leans her head back and thinks for a moment.

"This is where you say something to make me feel better," Aarik says.

"Better about what? I still don't really know what you feel bad about?"

"I dunno, maybe the fact that you had a full on relationship with a zombie boy. That your boo was a boo! Your goober was a ghoul, your zaddy was a zombie, a real ZILF."

"He's not a ghoul. Ghouls are living creatures that reside in the undercroft realm and feast on the the bodies of the dea–"

Aarik glares at her.

"Right, not the point." Ella clicks her tongue. "You have to understand Aarik, I'm not normal. As much as I don't like being called a weirdo and freak, I certainly live up to the expectations."

"Do you do it on purpose?"

"No. Yes–ut mostly no." Ella flip flops, and her head bobs back and forth. "I live my life on purpose. But I don't understand the world the way everyone else does. It just doesn't work like that for me. I was lonely, I met Xander, he was funny and caring, and for the first time in a long time I had a friend. To me there's nothing wrong with being friends with good people, and Xander is good people. It would mean a lot to me if you would try to be friends with him."

"You want me to be friends with a zombie?" Aarik looks at the lumbering silhouette walking toward them.

"I mean, he's only alive for a little bit longer, then he's back in the ground."

"And that's where he stays?"

"He'll be dead to me."

"Ella, he'll be dead to everyone." Aarik says as the sound of moaning fills the air. The death rattle echos and breaks out of the fog. Then Xander pops out of the white cold mist.

"Uuuuuuhhey Ella, how long is this gonna take, 'cause I'm feeling a bit peckish, and I see a quick snack."

"Go on we'll catch up," Ella says.

"Cool, cool, cool." Xander turns in a clumsy stiff way, then passes back into the gloom. His mewl acts as a signal to the other undead that he is joining their feast.

"See, he's like every other guy," Ella says. "From what I've seen, all men lead with their stomachs and dicks. And since his decayed a hundred years ago or so, I don't think he's gonna eat with his–"

"Hold up. First, gross. I don't want to know about his...you know li'l boogey. But he said he saw a snack?"

"Yeah, probably a bird or something. Maybe a rat." Ella says nonchalantly. Aarik holds up his finger, and looks around at the sky. The sound of moaning and groaning filling the air. As the chorus of undead compounds and rises in a song of terror.

Aarik hisses, "Do so many undead converge on a rat?"

"Not likely," Ella says. The sound of an explosion breaks the cool breeze and brings the two to their feet.

"That's one of Gwen's bombs," Ella says.

"Gwen's a snack, er, I mean, the snack." Aarik fumbles, then slows down. "Gwen is Xander's snack."

"Gwen's a snack?" Ella gives him a look of jealousy.

"You dated a zombie. You don't get to give me a hard time for thinking the barmaid is cute." Aarik runs into the haze, summoning his bow and escaping the slip of his tongue.

"Brohn! Brohn!" Moses shouts as he pushes Elliot

into the office.

Elliot protests as he fails his grapple check. "Moses, what's going on? What happened to that child?"

Moses continues to push Elliot into his office, while the boy stands staring at the two of them, the light flickering from the fire off his face. The conniving eyes, full of joyous trickery, the smirk of a prank well done.

"Brohn, can you please watch the child for a moment? Just gotta have a quick meeting," Moses says. Brohn looks up and sees the child standing alone. Moses and Elliot close the door behind them. Brohn throws down his towel and takes a glass of juice to the Maxius with a smile "Hey bud. It's ok, Moses will be back soon." His high pitched voice reached out in comfort. "You want some apple juice? Fresh pressed this morning."

Maxius turns slowly, as the eyes of possession beam outward. Brohn pulls back a bit and the child takes the cup from his hands. A feeling of terror runs down Brohn's spine. He watches as Maxius drinks the entire cup.

"This vessel thanks you for the sweet malus pumila concentrate, kind sir. Your face is that of a generous gentleman, and I will remember it when the Grimander Corp takes control of this place."

"You can just say thanks little man."

"What is that thing out there?" Elliot shouts at Moses.

"It's a child."

"No, Moses, no that is not. It's inside a child."

"Gross."

"I feel gross having said it."

"Calm down, Elliot, you're freaking out over nothing."

"NOTHING!? Something has happened to that child. Something is possessing him."

"Not something, someone? You know what? Yeah, not that big a deal, I got it all handled. Why don't you stay in here, and I'll go take care of it," Moses tries to leave. Elliot pushes the door closed.

"What is it, Moses?"

Silence.

"Moses."

Moses closes his eyes. He breathes in and steadies himself. "It's a Fey creature." He cringes waiting for an onslaught of verbal abuse. When none comes, he turns in confusion. Elliot looks down at the ground and thinks for a second.

"You're not gonna yell at me?" Moses asks.

"If it's just a fae, then I think we'll be ok."

"Really?"

"Yeah, they are mischievous creatures, but they follow a strict code of rules," Elliot says. He walks over to his books shelf and pulls a leather bound tome out. "Fae by the Numbers. This should have everything we need. Saint Youn's root, a four leaf clover, a daisy, some iron." Elliot flips through the pages and smirks, his curly blonde hair loose in his eyes. "This is great. As long as he's not an arch fae, then we have a chance at getting rid of him."

Moses hisses inward. He cringes in emotional pain.

"What?"

"So, this is one hundred percent an arch fae. That kind wants to make a deal with me."

Elliot throws his book down. "Are you trying to give me an ulcer? Did you spend the time I was gone thinking of new ways to make my brain explode?"

"A bit dramatic."

"No, Moses, no. This?" Elliot wiggles his pointer

finger back and forth between him and Moses. "This is not dramatic. What we're about to do to that child is dramatic. The way his mother will most likely murder us will be dramatic. But this?" Elliot wiggles again. Moses grabs the finger. "Let me show you dramatic, you doodlefop."

The fire in the fireplace burns with blue and green flame. The radiation casts out across Elliot, Moses and Brohn in black cloaks. Elliot holds out a book, while the other two hold amulets with eight interconnecting circles laid in gold and gems. Elliot calls out a great prayer of retribution and conviction, while sparks fly from candles and torches around them. In the middle of the three is Maxius, tied to a chair, rope gagging him, and his feet in two separate bowls. One is filled with honey, the other with milk.

Elliot finishes his incantation, and the candles shoot out violet dark flames. A wind rushes through the building, and the shadows creep about. "This, Moses, this is being dramatic!"

"You did what?" Sycilia shouts from the grave.

"I blew a couple of them!" Gwen watches the two sizzling corpses laying before her. She had indeed thrown a bomb, which killed several in the back, but caught a couple more on fire. As they came closer, she let loose a spray of fire directly from her hands. Their flesh cooked and melted, but they didn't fall. It wasn't until she lifted several broken gravestone chunks into the air and shot them through the zombies heads that they finally fell.

"Super easy."

"First of all, you blew them up. Up is a very important word in that statement. So the bombs worked?"

Sycilia asks, watching the zombie head in the grave with her, chomping.

"Yeah, well, as long as you destroy the brain," Gwen says. Sycilia stakes her blade through the head, and it immediately goes slack.

"Good work, Gwen," Sycilia says. "But you still need to get me out of here."

"I would love to, but we have more friends coming in." Gwen can see the silhouettes surrounding the small grave field where she stands. Her hands are on fire and several rocks float in the air, ready to attack the first undead she sees.

The shambling creatures come closer, feeling the air with their hands forward, led by their ears and noses. The promise of warm flesh pumping their legs forward. The wet in the air clings to the undead skin and pulls at old wounds. Blood drips from their fingers and teeth, a trail of their deeds.

"Here they come, Sycilia," Gwen says.

"You have to stand your ground, Gwen. You're one of the strongest people I've met and I have all the confidence in the world that you can defeat them all." Sycilia takes the body of the zombie apart, breaks the coffin below her, and slams the debris into the mud, hammering the bones and limbs with her sword.

Gwen hears a moan from behind her, turning in time to see a ghoul bearing down on her. In a split second a large rock flings itself at the creature's head, killing it with a snap of its neck, blowing out the brain. She screams and Sycilia shouts out.

"I'm coming, Gwen!" She hoists herself up on the body part ladder. She digs her blade into the mud and fights the spilling earth around her.

Gwen spins to see two more undead breaking out of the mist. She lets out a massive blast of fire, consuming the one on the right. The muscles and skin bake and melt, leaving it collapsed on the ground. The second launches for an attack, knocking Gwen down. She scrambles back while the zombie crawls like a skiddling animal toward her. She lets out a scream as he climbs over her body and unhinges his jaw to take a chunk out of her.

Suddenly the creature yelps and stiffins. Gwen watches as it falls to her right, then sees that an arrow protrudes from the back of the zombie's head. She looks up and sees Aarik knocking a second arrow. He releases it over Gwen and it sinks into a goober's forehead. The thing falls immediately and slides into the grave as Sycilia makes her way out the other side.

"Aarik!" Sycilia says as she grapples with gravity to get over the ledge. Aarik runs over and helps her out. Gwen takes Sycilia's blade, and in the quick moment of contact, for the second time in as many months, it feels like all the magic in her blood, the secret of her power, rushes out of her body. She feels normal and capable.

It feels like she is becoming coming she once was. Something different, something bigger than her. A bottle of whisky open within a lake. She feels good. Then, she casts a spell. It leaves her body and channels into the Sandren Blade. The magic sword stores the enchantment–it waits to use the spell she's given it. She then hands it to Sycilia.

"Thanks Gwen," Sycilia says.

"What about me? I helped," Aarik demands.

"Gwen almost died. She fought those things alone."

"Thanks, Aarik," Gwen says, running her hair back behind her ears.

"You're welcome, Gwen," Aarik says, bowing to the girl. She blushes. "What were you doing in a grave,

Syl?"

"I just thought it might be a good place to take a lunch break–you know, eight freaking feet in the ground."

"That seems absurdly deep," Aarik says, looking down into the ditch.

"This cemetery is hundreds of years old, possibly a thousand years old," Ella says, walking with Xander. "They bury people on top of others here. Then cover an area in dirt and let it sit for a hundred years or so, and fill the new layer of dirt. In the oldest parts of this place the coffins may stack a hundred deep."

"Hey, look it's Ella, walking with a zombie, like it's not a killing machine," Sycilia says in mock nonchalance.

"That's her ex-boyfriend," Aarik whispers.

"Your boyfriend died? And then got buried here?" Sycilia runs forward to comfort her friend.

"Conclave, I wish it was that way," Aarik says to Gwen after Sycilia runs to Ella.

"Actually," Ella begins, "He was already de–"

"It doesn't matter," Aarik says. "Doesn't matter, we can move on. She's fine, and not sad about anything that's happened in this cemetery ever. We can just move on. Xander here, yup, the zombie's name is Xander."

"Hello," Xander waves.

"Xander here is taking us to the big bad evil guy of this macabre quest, and I for one am ready to go. Gwen, would you like to get out of this realm of death and move on with our lives?"

"Yeah, to be honest, having to fight those undead really took it out of me," Gwen says.

"Syl, I'm guessing you're good, unless you want another dip in the ancient grave of what might or might not be someone's honey bun, sweet thang, or baby boo."

"I think I'm ready," Sycilia says.

"Great. Ella, would you please have your former paramore lead the way?"

"That was all very petulant, but apt," Xander says. "I can see why you like him." The zombie shambals forward and leads the group into the mist.

"Don't be nice to me Xander," Aarik. "You eat people's faces."

The three at the tavern have etched the runic symbol of the Hallowed Conclave into the ground and set it ablaze, leaving the wood scorched. Pages of books lay strewn about and the three of them breathe heavily while watching the child. Maxius muffles slightly. Despite being forced down and exercised, the child seems exceedingly calm. Brohn goes over to the rope and pulls it off his mouth.

"This is all quite unnecessary," The boy says. "I only wish to speak to you and discuss the possible acquisition of the pennmmmmfffhmm." Moses puts the rope back on the boy's mouth.

"Well, no need to listen to that monster's lies."

"Wait a minute," Elliot says. "This is all because he wants to talk to us?"

"Yeah, exactly, this creature cannot be trusted."

"No, Moses, we need to hear him out. That's the only way we can get him out."

"How?" Brohn asks.

"Do you promise that if I hear you out, you'll release this child from your domination?" Elliot asks Maxius. Maxius calmly nods his head.

Moses steps in front of Elliot. "You're gonna believe

him? He's a liar who takes control of children's bodies."

Elliot pushes past the paladin, sticks out his hand and says, "Do you pinkie promise?"

"Pinkie promise?" Brohn asks.

"If he breaks a pinkie promise, then I own everything his pinkie has ever touched," Elliot says. He then turns his attention to the child. "Do you pinkie promise?" Elliot's hand waits, pinkie extended out. Then the child's pinkie wraps around Elliot's.

"Wait, you could move your arm the whole time?" Moses jets in. "I tied those as box knots; you were never gonna get out." The boy pulls the rope from his mouth.

"I'm an arch fae, Moses Summerhill, ropes have become a form of recreation in my long years."

"Sounds fun," Brohn says quickly. They all look at him, and he shrinks back.

Maxius looks back at Elliot and smiles, despite being much shorter than the cleric, the boy seems to look down on the man. "I'm happy to tell you that I love what you've been doing with the place. As soon as you and Moses come to an agreement, I would love to bring you into th–" Then a sudden popping noise and the boy is gone. A quick flash and the magic takes its effect. The scent of bread wafts through the room. Brohn and Elliot glance at Moses who has a cut hair tied to two fingers.

"Did you just banish that child?" Brohn asks.

Moses throws his hands behind his back, looking guilty. "Uh, no. It must have teleported on its own. I mean, come on, it is an arch fae. They can kinda do what they want."

"Moses, what is wrong with you? You need to drop the spell now," Elliot demands, readjusting his glasses. “Bring that child back.”

“Seriously, Moses, that place is no joke,” Brohn says.

“He’s fine. I’ll bring him back when the arch fae leaves him,” Moses offers.

“You bring him back now.” Elliot whistles. A scatter and clanging comes from the kitchen and within a few seconds Potsticker comes running out. “If you don’t, I’ll sic Potsticker on you.”

“You wouldn’t dare,” Moses challenges. Elliot moves his eyes to Potsticker, who eagerly waits in the sink. As Elliot shifts his gaze back to Moses, Potsticker jumps in the air and grazes past Moses. Close enough to make the man feel a burn and yelp.

“Holy deity balls!” Moses shouts. He loses his hold on the spell and quickly the boy pops back into existence.

“Well that was a bit odd,” the boy says. Potsticker lands in the fireplace, and Moses recovers quickly. He then snaps his finger and pops the boy out of existence.

“Moses!” Elliot shouts. “Stop it!” Potsticker shoots a firespit at Moses. He curses and drops the spell.

“Please don’t do that--” Moses banishes him again. The child then begins the journey back and forth from reality to the ether. Everytime he comes back he sees a new scene.

Moses screams as Potsticker gnaws on his leg. Elliot running over to stop Moses. Moses snapping his finger.

Darkness.

The fire creature on Mose’s head burning his hair while Elliot casts healing magic. Brohn getting a pot to scoop up Potsticker. Moses snaps.

Darkness.

The tavern is on fire, Moses is being held by Brohn,

and Elliot begins casting a frost spell on the flames. Potsticker runs toward the child. Before the creature can make contact, Moses snaps.

Darkness.

Elliot has covered the entire tavern in ice and snow. Potsticker melts a bit of it from the fireplace and Brohn has tied Moses to a chair. Elliot walks up to Maxius, looks down, and cleans his glasses. "So you wanted to talk to us about something?"

"So you're like...a nice zombie?" Sycilia asks Xander. The group walks through the graveyard, passing by ancient mausoleums and statues of dead leaders. The roads grow easier to walk as the dirt pathways give way to old brick, then give way to well placed cobblestone.

Ella and Aarik walk next to each other while Sycilia and Gwen walk with Xander. Gwen watches the blade in Sycilia's hand; it glows slightly with the infusion of magic. The fact that Sycilia has yet to notice strikes Gwen curiously. No one notices the black line of magic that leads Xander through the cemetery.

"I'd say so. But most people think they're nice enough," Xander replies. "I was a nice person in life, and I think that carries over."

"But the other zombies," Gwen picks up the conversation, "try to eat people."

"I eat people. I could totally eat a person."

"Why don't you? I mean, why didn't you attack me like the others did?"

"Ella caught me before I did, and she told me you were friends."

"That's it?" Sycilia asks.

"What?"

"That's the only reason you didn't attack and try to

eat her?"

Xander thinks about it, his dead eyes rolling back and forth, he snaps his jaw in thought. "If you have a friend, and they have a pet rabbit, would you cook and eat it?"

"No," Gwen says.

"Why?"

"'Cause that rabbit belongs to somebody and they care about it."

"But rabbit is delicious and makes a very good stew."

"So what? Rabbits and humans are very different."

"I'm sure the rabbit would disagree."

"That's an animal."

"Which is why I'm guessing you never stopped to talk to one, ask how it feels about you eating its friends and family?"

"Well, no. I mean, yeah. I mean...." Sycilia trails off.

"So what?" Gwen asks. "We're just Ella's pets? That's why you don't eat us?"

"If that's how you want to see it. Then sure. Ella reminds me of who I used to be, so I'm happy to not eat her friends."

"You compared me to a pet rabbit," Sycilia says.

"Who were you?" Gwen presses.

"Hmm?" Xander groans, then smiles a slack jawed smile. "I was a ranger once. A hunter."

Gwen pushes. "Like Ella?"

"Ha, no. Not so much. I hunted animals, beasts. Things of the forest. Lived in Haberdashery woods a couple hundred years ago. It's hard to remember, kinda like a dream, ya know?"

"That must be hard," Gwen says. "To have to remember your life, knowing it's over now."

"Kinda."

Sycilia tilts her head. "Kinda?"

Xander stops walking. He's outlined by a dead tree, reaching out into the white and darkening gray sky. It frames his broken body and wretched existence. "There are worlds beyond this one, places where the consciousness goes after death."

"I thought the Conclave takes the souls of the dead into their realms."

"For the most part, yeah, but there are some in the Conclave that work differently than the rest. The Ninth God, for instance, is between all realms."

"There are only eight Gods," Gwen says.

"Yeah, I think your brain might be rotten," Sycilia says. "Eight moons, Eight seats at the Hallowed Conclave. Eight Gods behind the Divine Wall."

"Either way," Xander says, "when I was alive, my girlfriend pulled some strings and got me in good with one of the Deities on the Conclave, and I found myself working for him after death."

"Did you say you're several hundred years old? When did you date Ella?" Gwen asks.

"Couple years ago," Xander says.

"After you died?"

"There's a lot you don't know about Ella."

"Clearly," Gwen says.

"What's up guys?" Ella says as she and Aarik catch up.

"Just talking to your Zombie ex-boyfriend about the multiverse and the ninth god," Gwen says.

"There's only eight gods, Gwen," Aarik says pompously. "Everyone knows that." He sticks his thumb at her and gives a face to Ella. Sycilia puts her hand to her forehead in disappointment.

"Xander," Ella says, "I thought you were going to take us to the person responsible for bringing you and all the other zombies to life." A slick line of magic slips past the group. It's the first time any of them notice the faint bit of energy coming off Xander's body. It leads around the tree and in the direction they had been walking, disappearing into the fog of the evening.

"I am, Ella, dear."

"Then why have you brought us back to the D'qoury estate?" Ella steps forward watching the string of black pulsate toward the emerging mansion. As she comes out of the brickwalled cemetery grounds, wild with trees and harsh grass, she enters the well manicured lawn of Lady D'qoury. The mansion windows loom up from the grass, lit with torches and flanked with massive pyres at the edge of the property. Xander's black energy string adds to multiple more streaming into the woods, into the cemetery.

"We've seen those strings before," Gwen says.

The danger starts to dawn on Aarik and Sycilia, together they curse, "Dern it to heck."

Xander steps forward and points to the woman sitting on a lounging chair, a warm drink in hand, servants holding platters of food for her. She watches them approach. The dark tendrils of magic all converge on her, and when she waves her hand, they all follow to the ring on her finger.

Xander points to Lady D'qoury, his black line leading to the ring on his finger. "Lady D'qoury is the one that brought us back to life."

Maxius, the child under the care of the Penny Lich crew, sits with a glass of apple juice at the end of the bar. The evening crowd is now filling the tavern. Workers come in for the warm soup that Potsticker has been simmering in the back, while Brohn greets each new customer with a warm cider and some bread left by Hadvar before he left for the day.

"We have a few nice spots in the back there gentlemen," Brohn says as two new fellows enter, and Brohn sets a tray on a table for a few young ladies. One of them puts her hand on his strong arm as she thanks him, and the other two giggle. Brohn flashes a practiced smile, and goes back to work.

Moses leans against the bar and takes a swig of his drink. "Look, I don't think this is a good idea."

"I know," Elliot says, pulling out his book. A fluttering quill floats into the air and readies itself into position over the book. "Everyone can tell from the burn marks left from you trying to banish a child from our world."

"The burn marks are from your demon creature attacking me. You know how many healing points I had to use on myself?"

Elliot clicks his tongue in disagreement. Moses clicks back. They stare at each other.

"That is no divine magic," Maxius says without acknowledging the two.

"What?" Elliot asks.

"The pen." The floating quill above the page waits for Elliot's command. "The magic to command that pen is not divine; it comes from beyond."

"It's something I picked up in my studies in the Candle Crypts," Elliot says. "Most clerics learn it–that and a few other tricks."

"But you know quite a few more tricks than most, don't you Elliot of Denier."

The two men look at each other. Moses puts his finger to his throat and slices. Elliot shakes his head. Moses nods toward the child. Elliot ignores the signs, then waves his hand. The quill begins moving.

"What is your name?" Elliot asks, and the question is written down in the book.

Maxius looks at the quill and smiles. "I'm Grimander." The name is written down in the book and he watches the ink dry.

"You're an Archfey?"

Grimander thinks for a moment. "Yes."

"And what is it that you want?"

"Well, I think we're all good here, am I right?" Moses says moving forward. Elliot stops him and waits for the answer.

Grimander, moving Maxius's head, looks at Moses. "Several weeks ago, I began negotiations with Paladin Moses for the acquisition of this guild and fine establishment for my own corporation. We spoke of a great multitude of things, and I was left with the impression that he was going to speak to you about the decision to relinquish the Penny Lich and your associates to my management."

"And that's it, that's all we spoke about," Moses says, staring at Maxius.

Elliot looks at the words written on the page, studying what he had just heard.

"You...." Elliot tries but can't find the right words. "You want to sell the guild?"

"No, I don't want to sell the guild," Moses starts.

"It sure as shit seems like you want to sell. You went and found an Archfey to make a deal with. They literally write stories about how that's the worst thing you can do."

"No, that's not it. I just wanted to find us some options because I feel like we're both...." Moses thinks for a second. Elliot fills the silence.

"What? Both what? We finally start getting this place

going, we finally have something good in our lives, and you want to get rid of it? I don't understand; it makes no sense."

"We're close, I agree, but we don't have our own thing here, Elliot. Don't you see? We're still puppets for the Magecore. We take their jobs, we still both work for the temple, we still don't have the power to cut ourselves free."

"Cut ourselves free?" Elliot reels at the idea. "You want to...." He slides in and speaks quietly. "You want to leave the Magecore–the temple?"

Moses stays silent, shifting his eyes back and forth. He breathes in and answers, "Grimander's offer can help us. But I didn't know how to bring this up, and I wanted more time. I wanted to find the right moment to talk about it."

"Talk about desertion, heresy, treason? You just needed to find the right time for those conversations?"

"I don't mean to interrupt," Brohn says, "but it looks like Maxius's mother is here."

The two look at the door and see the same woman returning, bags in hand.

"Damnit," Moses says. "We can't send her home with some fae child."

"Brohn, distract her," Elliot says.

"How?"

"Kindness."

Ella, Aarik, Sycilia, and Gwen all make their way across the yard leading up to the D'quory manor. The somber chill night lets snow fall, crunching beneath their feet. Moans and guttural calls of the undead crawl out of the tree line from behind. The black tendrils of magic stream past the heroes and into the woods, each one tied to a corpse come back to life. The group stands a few feet in front of the lady of the estate. A cold Gaze wind blows between the groups, and Lady D'quory sips on her hot drink.

With all the energy he can muster into sounding as effortless and uninterested as possible, Aarik asks a simple question: "Why?"

"Why?" Sycilia asks.

"Why?" Gwen pushes.

Lady D'qoury turns to Ella, expecting the same question. Ella realizes that the others are watching her She looks confused and looks back at the lady. "You've been digging the dead up. For what purpose?"

"Or as we like to say in Haberdashery Woods," Aarik says, "Why!?'

The Lady of House D'qoury smiles, runs her finger around the rim of her drink, and looks Aarik up and down.

"When Waller first came to me, I was young and loyal to the kingdom. I was loyal to the MMistress and her ideals. But after what happened to Waller, I started to ask questions, and I realized he was right all along."

"Lady, we have zero idea what you're talking about," Aarik says. He summons his bow, and knocks an arrow, pointing it at the ground. "But I think it's time we take you to the militia to answer for your crimes."

"What crimes?" she asks.

"You–" Aarik stumbles on his answer. "Well, you brought people back from the dead. That's gotta be illegal, right?" He looks around at the others. "Right?"

Gwen speaks up, "Yeah, somehow. It's against, like... regulations of the code of, uh, cemetery...workers."

"These bodies have been brought to my family for centuries; we own what others refuse to keep track of."

"You use unlicensed and unsanctioned magic," Sycilia says, stepping forward. "The ring on your finger is dangerous, and I'm sure the Magecore would like to take a look at it."

The lady turns to Sycilia and smirks. "Magic is a right of the people. You can't control it; by its very nature it looks for ways to break free. I don't need the government to tell me when I can and can't use it."

"Maybe in you la la land you don't, but here in the real world, we have rules," Sycilia says, "There's no getting around them. Now I suggest you drop the ring, and submit yourself to arrest, else I'm going to have to use force."

"You fools, I wanted you to come here. I planned this. And outside of Ella's boytoy leading you back here, this is all going perfectly."

"Why?" Ella asks.

"Really? Now?" Aarik says indignantly at Ella.

"Because the Penny Lich Guild is nothing but a puppet of the Magecore. Your owners are still a part of the temple, they still answer to the Mistress. You are nothing but a nuisance to our plans. So I lured you here with a li'l quest. And now I will sick my army of undead on you."

The party looks back to see a massive line of half rotten monsters waiting to attack. Grime, ichor, viscous insides all dropping to the ground. Bloodstained mouths gasp and rasp on air to fill dead lungs.

"I have brought you here for one reason, and one reason only," Lady D'quory says. The small handful of servants around her begin dropping their platters and transform, dropping glitter magic to become seething undead creatures.

"Is it for sandwiches and tea?" Aarik asks.

"To die," Lady D'qoury says.

"Well that's not very creative," Sycilia says.

The servant zombies begin the attack, running forward, claws up. The party splits quickly. Aarik and Ella are first to let off shots. Ella throws a dagger from her hip at the closest one and lands the blade in the creature's chest. It continues to charge, and she spins out of its way. As it passes by, she pulls the dagger out and then places the edge in the back of the zombie's head.

Aarik lets two arrows loose in quick succession. The first lands in the creature's brain and drops it immediately. The second lands in its throat, causing blood and a croaking noise to escape from the man's mouth. It stumbles about. Aarik moves out of its way and leaves enough room for Sycilia to swing above him. The large black blade cuts the man in half. With a second swing she decapitates the monster.

Gwen throws a bottle of fire past Lady D'qory as the woman turns to flee the attacking party. The bottle shatters and erupts into a massive wall of fire. The warmth and light lick her face. Her smirk turns to anger and she wheels back to the guild.

"You fools, you think you can withstand all my minions? I am the Mistress of death! Every family in the kingdom has loved ones here. I have amassed an army to help break the Magecore and free the people of this kingdom. The New House will no longer wait for the Sandren's return. Waller was right, and I will make sure his legacy is–"

She stops speaking as Sycilia's blade stabs through her belly. Looking as surprised by the attack as the others, Sycilia lets go of the sword, and in that moment she can see the thing push its way into the woman farther.

She coughs blood and looks at them all. Her eyes

land on Aarik and she smirks. "If I'm going to go, then then I'm going to take one of you with me." She holds up her finger, the ring pulsating with magic. It shoots forward and hits Aarik.

Immediately he feels his body begin to age. As his soul is siphoned, he screams in agony. His skin grows pale and his muscles are gaunt., eyes rolling in the back of his head.

Lady D'quory laughs. "I suffer a little longer, taking your life and sustaining my own. All so that you may die and become my new toy!" Crackling in pain and joy, she stands, the blade still in her, the death finger unwavering toward Aarik. "I will have your lives, and soon the beast will awaken. It will let loose the magic of this valley! I will be queen and you will be my undead serv–"

A body steps between her and Aarik. The body of a once dead, now alive, but still mostly dead, ex-boyfriend.

"I got you, bro!" Xander shouts, as he takes the blast of D'qoury's magic. Aarik falls over, no longer being affected by the curse. As Xander stands heroic, the black and purple tendrils of magic whip about, pulling at his flesh. He lifts his ring and seemingly pulls back at the Lady of the estate.

"What, what are you doing!?" she screams. "Let me go! You'll kill me!"

"This was a terrible choice," Xander says. "I'm in an excruciating amount of pain!" Ella runs near him, "No! Elderberry, stop. I will take this on. I will be the hero you no, you know what, no I can't, I can't do it, I've made a terrible mistake. Oh, I can't stop, I'm commidtted now, I gotta do it."

"Let her go!" Ella says from nearby. "You won't resurrect if you keep this up. I won't, I won't ever see you again."

"I'll miss you, babe, but I've been waking up too often. It's time for me to actually get some rest." Xander turns back to Aarik. "Don't let her down, Aarik."

"What are you doing!?" the woman screams, hair flying about. "You'll kill us both! You fool, I command you to stop this! I'm your master! You must obey m–" Then she explodes.

Like super epicly, she's gone.

One second she's screaming at the zombie, then the next second it's guts, and blood, and vaporized skin expanding outward. The cold wind of Gaze picks up the light molecules of her body and transfers her to the air, leaving only the heavy viscera splashed about on the ground.

Aarik wakes up from unconsciousness screaming. "GLAAAAAH! Bad skin, bad skin. I'm a zombie, oh Divine, I'm a zombie!"

"You're not a zombie, Aarik," Sycilia says, helping him up.

"I am, I'm a gosh dern freaking zombie!"

"Stop it."

"Look, look at my walk." He hobbles about a little. "That's a shamble. I'm shambling now. Conclave no, I'm a shambler."

"Aarik." Gwen walks over. "You're not a zombie. You were saved."

"Nice try. But I know it, I know it. All I want to do is take you and ravage your supple body, Gwen."

"Inappropriate," Sycilia says.

"Shut up, let him talk," Gwen blushes and grins, swaying back and forth at the thought.

"And look, I can't feel pain. I can't feel anything. Oh my Deities no, I can't feel the warmth of a lover's touch," Aarik says. Sycillia rolls her eyes and pulls out her dagger. She quickly grabs Aarik's hand and, in a spot familiar to her, she stabs the blade into his flesh.

"MOTHER OF GRUBOUS!" Aarik shouts.

"You can feel it. You're not a zombie. Just brainless." Sycilia puts the dagger back in her belt.

"You gonna be ok, Aarik?" A voice asks from below. They look down and see Ella holding Xander–his body slightly repaired, skin growing back and hair less stringy. His half-elven features become striking, and his old self returns for a moment.

"Whoa," Aarik says, getting close to Xander opposite Ella. "Hey, you know you're pretty good looking when you're not mostly dead."

Xander laughs. "I'm glad you think so."

"Why'd you do that, Xander?" Ella asks.

"For you," he replies. "For him." He turns to Aarik. "I want you to take care of her. Don't let her down, you got it?"

"I do. I understand."

Xander does an insight check, eyes squinted, "No you don't."

"No, I have zero idea what you're talking about, but you're dying and you're very cute, and I don't want to let you down."

"Aarik, I'm already dead. Been dead for a couple hundred years. Ella, I'm gonna miss you, you know."

"I'm gonna miss you too," she says with tears in her eyes, but holding them back, and holding his hand. "You were a very good friend to me. It means a lot to me, you know."

"I know." He pulls her in and kisses her on the forehead., then rubs her hair. "I always had a thing for redheads, you know?"

Ella laughs.

"This is it, dying again, here we go." Xander leans

back and closes his eyes. "Argerlarger, here we go. Death and death again. I'm a pot of water, being let loose in the ocean. Floating away into a place where I am forever...."

Soon the wind of the cold month takes the spirit of Xander away into the unknown. The moons of Onto begin their conjunctions in the sky. Deep open dark skies are lit by the cosmic aurora shimmering in neon colors. The moons look down upon the world as Xander's spirit rises up to their ever watching Conclave. His shell is left for others as a reminder of who he once was.

"Hey there Ms. Maxius's mother," Brohn says, holding a warm mug of cider. "How'd the packing go?" She looks up and sees the brawny man offering her a drink and her eyes widen. A salacious smile crosses her face, "Perhaps you can take a few minutes and entertain a weary bartender."

"I think I can spare a moment for a warm drink," she winks.

"Ok good, Brohn's innate sexual magnetism is being put to good use for once," Moses says watching the scene from across the tavern.

"Grimander," Elliot says, "I regret to inform you that my business partner was a little rash in entering into conversations with your organization. We are not looking for any buyouts or takeovers."

"That is not the answer I was looking for," Grimander says. "And there is much that I have left to explain about this union."

Elliot takes the book and quill, and begins drawing on a new sheet of paper.

"We at Grimander Incorporated have a rich history

of working with local talent and agencies to complete jobs on a realm-wide stage..." Grimander continues to speak as Elliot draws. Moses watches Brohn drink with the boy's mother, and soon she sees Moses looking at her. She waves at him and stands up.

"Shit." Moses drops down in his chair. "By no fault of my own, that woman is coming over here."

"Hold on, don't you want to finish the drink?" Brohn asks, holding the woman's hand.

"I just want to say hi to Maxius and let him know I'm here. I saw Moses over there and figured they are together."

Brohn thinks for a second as the woman begins walking away. "Uh...I Uh..." Moses shoots him a look from the far side of the bar. "Buh, I'm uh...I love you!" Brohn shouts out. The tavern stops and the woman looks back at him.

"I'm in love with you...uh...Maxius's mom. From the moment I first laid eyes on you." Brohn stands up and walks toward her. The crowd swoons–some of the young women look on with jealousy. Some with hatred. "You are the fairest flower in the winter storm, a sight for weary eyes."

"You better wrap it up, Grimander!" Moses hisses. "Get out of that kid."

"We have a very competitive compensation and benefits plan. Some would say out of this world. Haha. That's a little joke." Grimander rambles on. "And we of course are a diverse and equal opportunity employer that looks for talent to rise up through the ranks. As well we would love for you to try out our–"

Elliot rips the page out of his book and slaps it on the boy's face. The glyph on the page glows and the boy's body convulses, as a black smoke leaves through his ears, mouth, and eyes. After a moment, the magic is done and the boy slumps over.

"Will you, my darling, my beautiful," Brohn continues, "will you take my hand, and make me the happiest man in all the realm of Onto?"

The room is silent as Brohn drops to one knee. The woman can't help but smirk. She shakes her head in confusion. "Ummmm...no thanks."

"That makes sense." Brohn stands up and wipes his knees off. The crowd waits. He looks around. "Well, I'm single again! Drinks on the house!" The crowd erupts and cheers for the man.

"What the hellsrealm was that?" Moses asks.

"As soon as he told me his name I knew that I recognized it. He's a servant of the ninth god. The Pact. That glyph is a Conclave Ward created by the Halt'Iari. It's an aberrant spell that banishes a deity from a house."

"The house being the boy's body?"

"Yup."

"Is he ok?" Maxius's mother asks as she reaches them. Elliot lifts Galador's head while holding the paper on the bar. Maxius wakes up as they bring his head up. He sees his mother and his eyes shoot wide open.

"Moma!" He says excitedly. He jumps up and runs to her.

"He's fine," Moses says. "Just had a bit too much of the warm cider. Sugar crash and all that."

"Oh, my boy," she says as she embraces her son. "I'm glad you're ok. We are just about ready to go. Are you excited for our trip?"

"Yeah,"

"Good, let's get going." She ruffles his hair and looks back up to the cleric and paladin. "How much do I owe you?"

Moses holds out his hand. "Hold onto your coin. Use it to help start a new life. To find some peace."

The woman smiles, and leans in, kissing him on the cheek. Moses feels a familiar longing for something that has eluded him his entire life. She pulls back, then looks over to Elliot. He holds a hand up to stop her from leaning into him.

"He did all the work. He can have mine."

"If you're ever in North Calstem, look me up," she says as she turns and takes her son out into the cold Gaze evening.

"Mama, I was in a big upside down building," Maxius says. "And a lady there told me all about how she fought a big jelly monster."

Elliot and Moses watch the two leave. As soon as they are out of the tavern, Moses snaps his fingers. "Shootpoop!"

"What?"

"I forgot to ask what her name was. Eh, I can just look her up as Maxius's mom, right?"

Elliot scoffs, closes his book and grabs the quill. He starts toward his office when Moses puts his hand on Eliot's shoulder.

"You still mad about that whole thing?" Moses asks. Elliot looks at him for a moment. He seems to struggle with something, then lets go of it.

"No, I get it. The little bit of freedom we have won has only made us want more, right?"

"I love the life we have now, really I do," Moses says. "But there's so much holding us back. And I know you long for more. I know you want to be free from the Candle Crypts and the expectations of being a cleric. I believe in you, you know. You're probably one of the coolest guys I know."

"I don't know about that,"

"Dude, you just banished an Archfey back to the Conclave. Don't pretend like that's not cool."

Elliot blushes. "Ok, it's a little cool."

"Yeeeeeah, there he is. There's cool-guy Elliot. Come on, let's get a drink. They're on the house."

"I'm the house–they're on me."

"Even better. Next round on this guy!" The crowd cheers, lifting their drinks to the sky.

Ella and Aarik walk back to the Penny Lich, hand in hand. Behind them, Sycilia and Gwen walk a little slower. Gwen watches the two ahead as they speak softly. Her face gives away her emotions of disgust, anger, frustration, and pity.

"Hey." Sycilia pulls Gwen's attention.

"Huh?"

"I'm not blind, ya know."

"What?" Gwen turns to her friend.

"I'm not blind. I can see what's going on."

"Nothing's going on," Gwen says with guilt in her voice. "I don't actually like him, you know. It's just a little crush."

"Wait, what?" Sycilia stops.

"What?"

"You said you had a crush,"

"I didn't say that, you said–"

"No, you said you have a crush. On who?"

"I would never. I don't even like men. You're crazy."

Sycilia looms over Gwen. "Who?"

"I never, I...I just...." Gwen gives up and nods at Aarik. Sycilia looks up and sees her brother walking with Ella. She then breathes out and shakes her head.

"I know him well enough. You don't want to put yourself through that."

"That's up for me to choose. You said in this life, I

get to choose."

"I did."

"Then I choose this path."

Sycilia steps back. She chews on her cheek for a minute, then pulls her sword out. "This blade, you know it's special."

"I do. Something about magic storage or something."

"Something like that." Sycilia inspects Gwen. "It's a magic sword; it holds magic in it that can be used later. I don't know anything about magic, honestly. That's his purview. So I don't know how this thing would have a spell charged on it. But something keeps going through my head."

"What's that?" Gwen says, trying to stay cool, nonchalant, not guilty.

"I didn't stab that woman. I wanted to. But I didn't. The blade pulled itself toward her like it was being directed. As if some kind of magic spell had moved it."

"Wow. I mean, crazy. Right? Super duper weirdo beardo."

Sycilia stares at Gwen for a moment.

Then another moment passes. Gwen begins to feel awkward as the large, powerful woman stares at her.

"So...should we go?" Gwen asks. She makes a move toward the others. Sycilia's hand shoots out and grabs Gwen. Quickly, Gwen is pulled into an embrace and Sycilia holds her close.

"I'm not blind, Gwen. I'm kinda dumb, but I'm not blind. But most of all, babe, I'm on your side."

Gwen is frozen for a moment. She then let Sycilia's warmth over take her, and she gives into the hug.

"Thanks, Syl."

T.W. CLAWSON

The Penny Lich

A FANTASY SITCOM

'Twas the Night of Semperlunas

The songs of Semperlunas are filled with mourning and joy. They speak of the dead, they call out to the souls of the departed. Hymns of pain and sorrow that fill the hollow griever at the death of a father or mother. The unrelenting horror at the loss of a child or sibling. Semperlunas brings a tears to the eyes, and the handkerchief to wipe it with. It is bitter sweet. Warm fires in the cold nights. Lights in the window in the long darkness.

Somehow, though, interwoven in the tyranny of loss is the ultimate joy. The hope of peace. Semperlunas carols bring crashing into the mind some undeterred faith to life. They trace the reality of letting the mortal coil go, only to be caught by the Creators. The moons in the night sky stretch out in a single line, and look down on the world. A reminder of the gods and deities of the Hallowed Conclave that wait for all men in the end.

The Penny Lich, in fashion with festivities, is decorated with colored torch coverings, hanging paper ornaments and a collection of evergreen foliage sewn together and draped around the hearth, bar, and windows. Frost crawls up the cold glass of the windows, while the warm interior melts it away.

Gwen, the barmaid, hums to herself a more upbeat semperlunas carol–one about two lovers who died the year before. Him in battle, her by childbirth. After waiting a year at separate deity's realms, they return on semperlunas night to be with their child, together one more time as a family. She hums it with joy and beauty as she finishes decorating a cup: etchings of stars, evergreen trees, snow, and gravestones.

"Honey, it's too much," Hadvar says as he comes out of the kitchen. He brings with him several large bowls of warm stew and breakfast foods.

Gwen runs to help him. "What are you talking about? It's semperlunas! It's the most magical day of the year." She takes a bowl and puts it on the serving table covered in evergreen decorated cloth.

"I know you get excited every year, but you need to remember this holiday came to us from the Virgil Empire, and it celebrates magic. You need to–"

"Keep my mind on the world around me, I know. But dad, that's all we do. Before the guild bought the place–"

"Won it in a duel."

"Sure, before the guild show'd up, we only had stupid drunks and bandits running this place."

"Those stupid drunks and bandits kept us employed, food in your mouth, and a roof over your head."

"Yeah, but now the guild is doing that. And they're all good people. Elliot's the nicest guy ever, and Sycilia is strong and so cool. And then there's Aarik...." Her eyes flutter.

"Uuuuuuh, ok," Hadvar says. "I get it, you're your

own woman, and you're going to do your own thing. I'm all for that, but things are moving so fast out of nowhere. You move in with your friends, and then I find out you went on a quest the other week."

"You found out about that?" She looks scared.

"Yeah. Elliot's nice, which makes him easy to intimidate."

Gwen snaps out of uncertainty and into defense. "What did you do?"

"Nothing, I just asked him where you were and he snapped. It was really funny actually. Look, I'm just saying, you're old enough to do your own thing, I get it. Just don't go overboard and forget about your dear old dad. I've only had a few years with you and I don't want to see that come to an end."

"Dad," Gwen says, moving in for a hug. She nuzzles her face up to his chest and his heart melts. "I've been so happy ever since I came to be with you, you know that right?"

"Slightly aware of it."

"And I love working here with you, I just...." She slides back and looks at him. His face turns to concern.

"What is it, dew drop?" he asks with sudden uncertainty.

"I just, I'm learning who I am a bit more, you know?"

"In what way?" A grave look of concern runs across his face. Flashes of the past filter through his eyes as the sound of burning fire crackles around him. The egg, the egg, the egg, the egg, the egg.

"Like, my personality and who I think I want to be," Gwen says.

Hadvar snaps out of his terror and back to his daughter. "Oh, right. Of course."

"What did you think I meant?" Gwen asks.

"The egg. Er, I mean, nothing."

"What?"

"I got you a gift," Hadvar changes the subject. Gwen's eyes narrow in suspicion. She stares at him for half a minute and he can feel her insight check on him. She then breaks the investigation and cheers up.

"Well don't just tease me," she says. "Give it!" She holds out her hands and waits. Hadvar grabs a box from under the bar and puts it in his daughter's hands. She looks at him for a moment then turns her attention to the gift.

"It was your mothers," Hadvar says as she opens it. "She, uh, well she doesn't need it anymore, and I've always been afraid to give it to you." Gwen looks at the necklace in awe. A wide collar necklace with a single gem. The embossed design mixes vines and floral patterns with something like octopus tendrils. The gem shimmers in the light of the tavern, shifting from purple to green.

"This..." Gwen stares at the gift. "This was moms?"

"Yeah. I uh, I thought if you're going to start going off on adventures and stuff, then you might want to have it. She said it saved her life a few times, so, you know.... It's kinda good luck."

Gwen looks at it carefully and smiles. A tear fills her eye.

"What in the hellsrealms happened to the ceiling!?" Moses screams. He and Elliot walk in, and stare at the ceiling of the tavern. Looking down on the patrons is a ceiling now covered in an assortment of masks–heir gaze looking down on Elliot and Moses.

"What are those?" Elliot asks calmly, but visibly shaken.

"That's the Conclave Gaze," Gwen says.

"It looks like we're being invaded by a cast of demented bards," Moses says. "Do we have to keep them up there?"

"It's tradition. It's a part of the semperlunas celebration."

"We didn't ask why you did it; we asked if it has to stay," Elliot says.

"Yes," Hadvar says. "They stay. No other owner has cared." Gwen looks at him and he winks at her. Elliot slowly looks up, the conclave faces staring down at him. He breathes out as he gives up.

"Yeah, yeah, it's fine."

"What?" Moses exclaims. "I don't want the entirety of heaven looking down on me while I party tonight."

"This is their place, too, Moses. And if this helps Gwen celebrate semperlunas, then she can do it. Plus she's already done all this fantastic work–look at it."

"I'm looking," Moses says, staring at the ceiling.

"Here," Gwen says, holding a box for Moses and Elliot. "Maybe this will help you get into the spirit of semperlunas."

"What's this?" Moses looks at his box with discretion.

"A gift you dumbass," Gwen says. She thrusts it into his hands and gives Elliot his. They rip the paper and break into the boxes, pulling out a pin for each. Made of what looks to be pure gold, a circle like bending wood surrounds a hooded skeletal figure, who holds out a pint glass. old coins fall from his hand. It is intricate and beautiful.

"I found a local smith who makes guild and house pins and had him make these for you. I thought, as the leaders of your own guild, you would need to present yourself accordingly." Gwen walks over and pins the gift to Elliot's blue scarf around his neck. The light of the room flickers off it and matches his glasses as he holds his chin high and smiles.

"Oooh, me next," Moses says, handing the pin to Gwen. She grabs a leather strap that connects his shoulder plate to his chest and slides the decoration on.

"There you go. I'm realizing now I should have gotten yours in silver to match your eyes."

"Nah, this is cooler. Pure gold," Moses says.

"Well, I couldn't afford pure gold it's actuall–"

"Pure gold pins," Moses interrupts.

"No, Moses," Elliot says, "she's saying they aren't–"

"PUUUURE...GOLLLDA!" Moses demands.

"What's pure gold?" Sycilia asks as she, Aarik, and Ella walk into the bar.

"My winning smile," Aarik says.

"Your smile is mostly teeth, so I'm pretty sure your smile is pure enamel and gum," Ella says.

"No, Ella, that's not the saying," Aarik says.

"What saying?" Ella asks.

"A smile of pure gold."

"That's not a saying," Brohn says from a table. He works on a bowl of hot breakfast stew, his feet up on a second chair as he leans back.

"When did you get here?" Hadvar asks Brohn.

Brohn wipes stew from his auburn beard. "Been here the whole time, boss."

"What? No you haven't."

"It absolutely is a saying," Aarik interrupts. "He's flashing that smile of pure gold. That's a saying."

"No, I think I agree with Brohn," Sycilia says. "I don't think anyone has ever said that."

"It doesn't matter what you agree with," Aarik retorts. "I have heard people say it, and not just say it, they said it about me." He looks to Ella with a plea written on his face. "You think I have a pure gold smile, right babe?"

"Babe?" Ella questions. "We're babe now?"

"You're babe now?" Elliot raises his eyebrows.

"Babe?" Gwen rolls her eyes.

"Well, I just, I was just trying it out, you know?" Aarik says. He turns to the rest of the group, "We're gonna go on our first date tonight."

"So that makes you babes, then?" Moses asks.

Aarik shuffles. "No, I mean...unless you want to," he asks Ella. She gives an awkward face.

"Wait, what about our semperlunas party tonight?" Gwen asks. "You have to be there. It's our first one ever."

"Well–" Aarik cringes. "I know, and we'll try to make it, I just, I made some plans for a really special night, and you know when good ole Gold Smile takes you on a date, it's gonna be magical. You know what I'm sayin'?"

"First of all," Sycilia says, "don't ever call yourself 'good ole Gold Smile' again. Secondly, this is our first semperlunas together too, you know. Can't you cancel your date, just for tonight?"

Aarik looks at Ella–he's unable to read her face–as she works on getting herself some food. She seems to be completely unaware of the conversation, but Aarik knows the truth; she hears and sees everything. She's just giving him a chance to make the right choice.

"Sorry, I kinda made these plans without realizing the date. I'm sure we'll be back before the party is over," Aarik says.

"Oh, come on, man." Gwen says. "You're gonna miss out on the best drinks of the year."

"That's right," Hadvar says. "I'm gonna finally come out of the kitchen and make drinks. Show you guys all how a real cocktail is made."

Gwen spins. "What? No. I'm making my new recipes. The ones I've been working on all year."

"Haha, ok honey, but just remember who taught you to make drinks, ok?" Hadvar says as he puts his hand on her shoulder.

"Brohn?" Elliot asks. Hadvar quickly turns to him with a glare of disapproval. A shiver of fear runs down Elliot's spine. "I mean, uh, of course,"

"Nah bro," Brohn says standing up. "I learned from the streets. I make drinks that put hair on your chest."

"No thanks," Sycilia says.

"Look, I appreciate that you two take your jobs seriously," Hadvar says walking behind the bar and throwing a towel on his shoulder. "But I'm the king of cocktails. So, dew drop, you have fun hosting the party, and I'll make drinks, how does that sound?"

"Like a challenge," Gwen says. The guild gasps.

Moses pounds the bar rhythmically. "Fight, fight, fight, fight."

Sycilia pushes Moses, one of the few people physically capable of pushing his large frame backward. "Shut up. They aren't gonna fight."

"That's right," Gwen says. "We're gonna have a cock off."

"Nope," Aarik says. "That's not gonna be what it's called." The group hisses in disapproval.

"A drink off?" Ella asks.

"Boring," Aarik says. "Plus, that makes it sound like they're gonna drink. They are just making the drinks. We're the ones drinking them."

"So you're gonna stick around?" Gwen asks.

"Oh, sorry, I meant, they're gonna drink them," Aarik corrects.

"Lame," Gwen says. "So the rest of you will be here

for the challenge of the tails!"

"Ohhhhh, Sorry hon," Sycilia says. "I'm actually working a job for the first part of the day. Don't worry, I'll be back for the party though."

"What? So it's just gonna be Elliot, Moses, and Brohn?" Gwen asks.

"I'm actually taking Elliot with me," Sycilia grimaces. "Plus, you don't want him judging your drinks–he sucks at drinking."

"What?!" Elliot shouts as he eats some breakfast, "I'm very good at drinking. I know the wines, and ales and the...shooters and...."

"You're the worst bar owner ever," Ella says.

"Hey!" Elliot points at her with his spoon. "I can't refute that, so I'm just gonna ignore it." He turns back to Gwen. "But, yeah, Sycilia wanted help on this job, so I said I'd join. But Gwen, this soup is fantastic."

"I made the soup," Hadvar says.

"Oh.... Well, that's not good news for Gwen, 'cause this is really good soup."

"IT'S NOT A SOUP CONTEST!" Gwen shouts. "We're down to Moses and Brohn."

"Nope!" Brohn stands up. "I will not stand by while my honor is being besmirched."

"Spell besmirched," Moses says.

"Spell 'your mom'," Brohn says. "I am throwing my name in this goblet of fire water."

"What?!" Gwen throws her hands up. "So you two are going on a stupid date, in the freezing cold Gaze weather. And you two are doing some work, on the most holy day of the year. And I'm left here with my geriatric father."

"Hey!" Hadvar shouts.

Gwen silences her father with a finger, then points to Moses, "And mister broth beard over here, all so we can make our most special cocktails for one dude!?"

"Sounds like a beautiful way to celebrate semperlunas," Moses says, folding his hands behind his head and leaning back.

Yonder Valley evergreens line the streets of Valeward. Sitting outside in the snow, their frosted tips and frozen stems glisten in light of the new Gaze day. Colorful decorations contour the shapes of homes, lofts, and businesses around the city. Paintings of loved ones who have died are placed in windows. A soft flurry of white precipitation fills the air, along with songs of mourning and joy.

"The songs are so sad," Sycilia says as she walks with Elliot.

"Are they?" Elliot asks, looking at the groups of carolers. Some sing as they display pictures of dead family, or hang decorations, and others carol with worship, prayer, and hope that the Conclave hears them. "I guess I've just tuned it out you know? It is what it is."

Sycilia sticks her hand out and catches several flakes of snow. "You don't care for the holiday?"

Elliot studies her for a moment–er large frame, carrying the massive sword on her back. She could crush skulls; she could kill anyone. Yet she holds a fragile flake of snow, dark skin in contrast to the white precipitation. She is unique amongst the common, the drabble of the world. Her eyes glitter in wonder and awe. Elliot palms the box in his pocket and begins to summon the strength. Maybe she'll see it for the gift it is, maybe she wont understand, maybe she won't care. What if she knows and understands, but rejects it? His strength wanes.

"Do you?" Sycilia turns to him with her perfectly sculpted face. Strength behind beauty.

"I uh, I'm not so sure." Elliot says, trying to seem nonchalant.

"What? This is one of the best days, or rather, nights in the four hundred days of the year."

"If you say so."

"Why are you so cynical about this stuff?" Sycilia asks.

"What do you mean?"

"Come on, dude. Like when you had to officiate a wedding, or anything that has to do with the Conclave. You're like, extra shut off when it's these good things."

"I don't shut off."

"Seriously?"

"Yeah," Elliot says indignant, letting go of the box in his pocket.

"Tell me why you love Semperlunas," Sycilia challenges.

"What? Why?"

"'Cause if you're not shut off, then you'll have no reason to avoid the question."

"It's not really a question, it's more a demand. See a question has to rise up at the end. Like this?"

"You're avoiding the question?" Sycilia mocks.

"I'm not?" Elliot continues.

"Then why don't you answer? What's your favorite part of the day?"

"I think it's just a loaded statement, you know? Like it requires so much"

"Now, would be a good time." Sycilia crosses her arms.

"Gah!" Elliot rolls his eyes and puts his hands on his hips.

"Avoidance, dismissive body language." Sycilia points at him. "What's next, stonewaller? Gonna leave the conversation without a word?"

Elliot stands for a moment.

Sycilia begins, "Or are you gonna be a man and answer the damn qu–"

Elliot walks away.

"Hey!"

The brisk walk forces the cold air on his face, and Elliot pushes through the snow. He feels like he got away from the conversion, feels good about his escape, when a large feminine hand grabs his shoulder.

"Nope!" Sycilia says.

"Come one Syl." Elliot spins and faces her.

"Come on yourself,"

"Gross."

"Yeah, I heard it." Sycilia stands battle ready, "You might be able to get away with that shit with other people, but you and I are.... I mean to say...that we...."

"What?" Elliot looks intrigued. "We're what?"

"I mean, we're friends, obviously. But like–"

"Like what?" Elliot asks softly. He can see something, something she is avoiding. Something she can't express, not yet. Something that scares even him. He changes the subject.

"I was forced into the life of a cleric, Sycilia. I never chose it. You know?"

"Oh, shit it's happening," Sycilia whispers in disbelief. She leads him to a small cafe. They sit below an awning as the inside fireplace blasts heat out to the cold seating.

The Second Breakfast Cafe is where most first dates take place, or rather, most clientele of the cafe are first dates. It's noncommittal. Are they just getting coffee and testing the waters? Or are they going to get a little food and actually have a date? Maybe they take a booth and run the clock on this joint–do breakfast, lunch, and then hang for some dinner. Afterward, go back home together and work it all off. Maybe they just use the bathroom for a quickie and move on.

Please don't use the bathroom for a quickie; the staff has to clean up afterward and they are very tired of that happening.

Either way, The Second Breakfast staff is very good at picking up the subtext of a couple on their first date. They understand when there's attraction–a little flirting and hand holding. They know when a good date will sour, or even when the bad date turns good. Just not so good it ends up in the bathroom, please for the love of the Hollowed Conclave, stop using their bathroom for hookups. They serve food; it's a sanitation issue.

But the staff has never seen a date as silent and uncomfortable as when Aarik and Ella sit at their table. The sound of eating is overwhelming: scraping forks and knives, sipping of coffee and water. Someone thought that Aarik was going to reach down and retrieve a gift for Ella at one point, but he just needed to scratch his ankle. It was very disappointing.

"Don't do it, please don't do it," one of the servers begs the hostess. But she can't stand it anymore and needs to help these two. "You have no idea what it's like," another busboy says to the woman on her way to the awkward table.

"Did you guys know," the hostess says, "that we have a very nice bathroom, if you, uh...need to uh, use it. Very comfortable and, uh, private."

"Oh," Aarik says confused. "Thanks for that random piece of information."

"Yup, anytime," the girl says. She then puts the check on the table. "No rush, just whenever you're ready."

"Actually, I think we're, uh, I mean maybe we want to uh, Ella?" Aarik point's at Ella. She looks up from her knife, reflecting light off the blade. "Would you like some dessert?"

"Uh." Ella tries to find interest in the question. "Sure. Yeah. Sounds good."

"Great, so uh, two deserts," Aarik says.

"I'll send your server over right away." She takes the check with a snap.

"This is, uh–" Aarik rubs the back of his head. Ella looks up at him. He feigns a cough, and Ella looks away. Aarik deflates.

"What is going on?" Aarik asks, frustrated.

"What do you mean?" Ella doesn't look up.

"I mean, look, I'm really good at dating. I've done it a lot. Like if they had professional dating, I would be the boss of that."

"It's called prostitution."

"Ok, well, yeah, alright. Always good to be compared to a whore," Aarik says.

"No, I wasn't saying you're a harlot, just that that profession exists."

"And here I am bragging about being good at it."

"No, I love hearing about how good you are at seducing and courting other people," Ella says indifferently.

"Here's the problem–I can't tell if that's sarcasm or not."

"That's the problem?"

"Are you mad at me?"

'Why would I be mad at you? You've not said anything to me this whole time."

"Is that...."

"Yeah! Sarcasm. I'm capable of being sarcastic. If you're so good at dating, and courting, and being with people, then how come you suck at it with me. I was really looking forward to hanging with you."

"I was looking forward to hanging with you!"

"Then what the gosh dernnit is your problem."

"It's just, we normally talk about things like magic and adventure and how you use to date a zombie. And like, how you cast a memory wipe spell on Sycilia."

"You heard about that?"

"Elliot told me. He's like the biggest gossip in the entire guild."

"That jerk."

"I just–I have a hard time talking to you about, you know...normal stuff."

"I like talking to you about everything," Ella says.

"I like that, too." Aarik reaches out and takes Ella's hand. They stare into each other's eyes for a moment. Then Ella looks past Aarik, her eyes flutter, and then she snaps back to him and down at the table.

"So, what do you want to talk about?" Ella asks.

"I uh, like...you're...body? Ulgh." Aarik palms his head. "I'm sorry." Ella chuckles. "I'm sorry, I don't know what that was.

"This is hard when I'm in a place I'm not used to, you know?" Ella says.

"Yeah, I do. Like the Penny Lich would actually be a good place to be on a date right now."

"Yes!" Ella gets excited.

"And, you know...booze helps so much."

"So much," Ella agrees. "It's like my go to for talking to people."

"Me too!" Aarik puts his finger to his nose. He calms down and thinks for a moment. "And they are doing that drink contest thing at the Lich. Lots of booze,"

"In a familiar place...."

"Wanna go on a date with me back at the Penny

Lich?"

"I would genuinely love nothing more than that." Ella stands up.

"Well then, it's a date." Aarik stands up drops several coins on the table and collects his jacket. They take hands and begin walking toward the door. As they prepare to leave they're stopped by a person walking in. Their smiles drop as they see entering the cafe is the Mistress.

Moses sits at a table with three drinks in front of him. He looks them over, then up at the three people watching him watch his drinks.

"So...," he says.

"So, here we have the first round of drinks," Gwen says. "Your task is to fill out this form." She hands him a piece of paper with lines and graphs that he doesn't understand. "You're going to be telling us what you think of the taste, quality, and overall character of these drinks."

"How am I supposed to fill out this character sheet? I don't understand it at all?"

"No one does the first time they have to do it," Gwen says.

Moses sways back and forth, trying to wrap his head around the task. "How about I just drink them and tell you what I think?"

"No, this has to be a fair competition. The best way to do it is with anonymity and objective appreciation for each dri–"

"That one's mine!" Brohn says.

"Brohn, dammit!" Gwen throws the papers on the

ground.

"Hey, don't use my name in vain, lady," Brohn says. He then points at the drink in the middle. "This is what I call the Brown Note."

"Why?" Moses asks.

"Well, it's gin, vodka, silver rum, mezcal–"

"Those are all clear liquors," Moses says.

"Exactly, and then I add just a little bit of chocolate."

Moses takes the glass and holds it to his nose, and sniffs. "Good Deities above, it smells awful."

"Smell has nothing to do with taste–just drink it," Brohn pushes.

"What? Yes, it does. Half of your flavor comes from the smell of s–"

"Drink it, you bitch!" Brohn shouts.

Moses throws the glass back and lets some of it slide down. He slams the glass on the table and looks off for a minute. Brohn nods in anticipation.

"So," Brohn says, "what do you think?"

Moses nods his head, seemingly in approval, then points at Brohn, "You are immediately disqualified."

"What?"

"And If I ever find out you've made this for some unsuspecting victim, I'll haul you down to the magecore for treason."

"Come on, it's not that bad," Brohn says.

"Brohn, that tastes like a glass bottle exploded in my mouth because it was overfilled with rabies."

"Harsh."

"Seriously?" Hadvar asks. "It's that bad?"

"By all means...." Moses offers the drink. Hadvar takes it and flinches as he sniffs. He takes a swig and immediately spits it out.

"Immediately, you're fired," Hadvar says.

"Come on," Brohn argues.

"Immediately gone. You owe me money for trying this. It tastes like I've been breastfeeding off a zit."

"Good lords," Gwen says. She takes the drink, throws it back. Immediately letting it pour back into the glass. "You're a terrorist."

"It's not that bad," Brohn says.

Gwen pours the drink down the drain, "Brohn, this tastes like you captured a bunch of fairies, ripped their wings off, and threw them into a dragon's butthole."

"That's not even a flavor profile," Brohn says.

"You're forever disqualified from new drinks, forever and ever, amen," Hadvar says.

"Your children are disqualified," Moses says. He then turns to the other two. " So who's next?

Sycilia and Elliot sit at the outdoor table while the warm air from inside the Lucky Unicorn funnels outward. Two mugs of hot liquid steam in front of them.

"Stuff like Semperlunas are relics of times when people needed them to get by. But we've gotten to a point in society where we don't need them anymore," Elliot says, while Sycilia sips on her drink. "Being stuck in the Candle Crypts and then being forced to do the magecore's bidding, I finally have a chance to live my own life. And I've never had family, or a real reason to celebrate these holidays."

"You never exchanged gifts with Moses or Ella?"

"Ella and I exchanged gifts a few times as kids. She would usually give me something from some monster she killed, and I'd give her a story I wrote while in class. But once I went down into the magecore basement, I didn't really see the point. And Moses is great, but he's not the gift giving kinda guy."

"That's sad."

"Is it?"

Sycilia puts her drink down and twists it so it sits perfectly in front of her. "Before Aarik left Valley Gate, our family would have these massive festivals on our estate. My father would bring in gnomish trinkets from Polaris and we would hang them on every tree on the property. It took a whole week."

"Sounds exhausting," Elliot adds.

"It was. But, like, in the best of ways. Afterward, we'd go home and our mom would make spicy soup and hot cocoa. We'd sit by the fire pit and our uncles would tell us ghost stories. We found out later that they weren't actually ghost stories, but the stories of Semperlunas visits. That's why it's hard for me to hear the mourning in the Semperlunas songs here in Valeward. In Yonder Valley, our songs and stories are joyous and filled with gratitude to the deities of the Conclave."

"What happened after Aarik left?" Elliot asks, taking a drink.

"What?"

"You said all those nice things happened before Aarik left. What was Semperlunas like after?"

Sycilia takes a drink. She watches the dark liquid swirl as she sets it back down. Clicking her tongue, she looks up.

"I was a part of a gang. I was at one point the leader of said gang. And every year, we brought everyone back to HQ, and celebrated together. We would do 'Quiet Visitor' and everyone would get a gift from someone else in the gang. I still loved the night, because I still celebrated with my family. My new family."

Elliot turns his head in question, then fingers at the box in his pocket. "You love it that much?"

"I do." Sycilia chuckles. "I know it's childish, and I

know you were forced to celebrate it, but now that you have a choice to, wouldn't you be happier if you enjoyed it with the people you love?"

The question lingers in the air. The warm word hangs in the chilled space between them.

Love?

Love.

People, plural. Nonspecific. Royal Love. Elliot lets go of the box.

"I don't mind spending it with people, I'm just not sure there is much point for me to celebrate. I don't even have someone to wait on for a visit. My parents died when I was a newborn. I was given to the House of Denier to work at their temples."

"Semperlunas is about more than the dead coming back for one night to visit. It's about cherishing those around you now." Sycilia smiles. She then lifts the mug and throws back her drink. Quickly standing up, she grabs Elliot's scarf. "Come on, it's time for your gift."

"But my drink." He grabs at the drink and tries to drink it while being pulled, "And what about the job we were supposed to do?" He spills a little as Sycilia lets go of him. She rounds him, grabs the mug from his hand and downs the hot drink.

"That was still steaming hot," he says, watching.

She finishes the drink, placing the mug on the table, matching the same direction she put hers, "Yeah, that was a huge mistake. Now let's go!"

Brohn and Moses sit at the table with two drinks each.

"Gentlemen, before you is the first of my drinks," Hadvar says. "A drink that you can sip on throughout the night. Once you have obtained your buzz, it will help it sail forward like waves to a ship. This is Warm Apple Crisp."

"I'm not gonna lie," Moses says, "that sounds amazing."

"What's in it?"

"I start with a distilled and fermented cider made from apples here in Valeward. I then add a shot or two of high proof whisky. The sweet cider blends with the smoky and refined spirit. I then add some sugar and cinnamon to help create a fine bite that lingers in the mouth."

The two judges take sips of their drinks and feel the sweet apple flavor fill their senses. It washes down as the cinnamon tingles and pricks at the back of their throats. A spicy swelling runs up their noses as the whiskey hits their bellies and boils into a warm sensation throughout the body.

"My word, Hadvar," Moses says. Brohn breathes through a wide open mouth, releasing the heat from inside.

"This is like Semperlunas in my mouth."

"Like my dead parents came back from the dead and hugged my tongue," Brohn says.

"Like someone planted an orchard in my belly and the apples grew from my body and then melted directly into my brain."

"Like the first woman I ever made love to while simultaneously eating an entire pie."

"So you guys like it then?" Gwen asks, annoyed.

"Yeah, I'd say so," Moses says, drinking some water to clear his palate.

"Great, well enjoy it while you can 'cause once you have this, you'll never drink my father's swill again." Gwen puts down two glasses filled with inky black liquid. A couple bubbles pop as they rise to the top. Both men look at it, then back up at Gwen. She watches them intently. Slowly, they curl their fingers around the glasses and grimace. They look at each other and clink glasses, hesitating as long as possible. Anything to keep from having to put the cocktail in their mouths.

"Hon," Hadvar says lovingly, "it's honestly cute that you want to be like you dad, but I think it's clear that experience is going to overcome any new fandangled dri–"

"Oh my outer gods!" Moses says.

"What have you done?" Brohn asks in surprise.

Together they mutter out incoherent words and reactions. They point to Gwen. "Shes, ghlad. Ohmgawd. She's win. All win to her. Glamorous. Sweet nectar. Hadvash. Gorgonzola."

"What?!" Hadvar demands, "How does she win?"

"I dunno, man," Moses says. "Hers is better."

"No, Impossible, I spent the last decade perfecting that drink."

"It's cute you want to be like me dad, but you should leave the drinks to capable hands, eh?"

The two judges drink and spit out incoherent praises: "Capable, howdy dooda. Shleepy pinstripes in my brain. Great Fire Spiders! Yes sir, miser."

Hadvar looks frustrated. "Let me try that." He goes for Brohn's drink, but Brohn pulls back. He looks offended.

"Gutteralls!" Then Brohn downs his drink.

Hadvar turns to Moses. The paladin looks scared, mutters "Ditto," then downs his drink.

Hadvar crosses his arms and thinks. "Fine." He looks at Gwen, a smug look on her face. "Double or nothing."

"What?"

"Another drink," Hadvar says. "You win again, you'll be cocktail master of this place and I convince Elliot to give you a raise. If I win, you have to do the dishes for a month."

Gwen thinks about it for a moment, the sight of the judges scraping the glasses for more liquid makes her laugh. "Deal."

"Hello you two," the Mistress says.

"Mistress Evergreen," Aarik says, "good to see you." He takes note of her tight bun, and tighter hair style. Her clothes are near perfect–high collar and regal. The only blemish is the melting snow on her shoulder.

"How are you, Mistress?" Ella asks, looking her directly in the eye.

"I'm well."

"Here for a date?" Aarik smirks

"No, no," she says. "Far too busy for a date, I'm afraid."

"Really?" Aarik pushes. "So you came to the hottest date spot in Valeward by yourself. You really think we're gonna believe that you're that sad and pathetic? That you, lady of House Evergreen, royal patron of the magecore, are here to eat a solemn meal all by your lonesome on Superlunas, one of the most festive and wonderful days of the year. That you have zero people in your life to fill that empty hole for even a two hour lunch date?"

The hostess approaches from behind Aarik and holds up a menu. "Hello Mistress Evergreen. Table for one, as usual?"

Aarik's eyes are wide in shock and embarrassment.

"Yes, thank you," the Mistress says calmly, looking over Aarik. "Now, if you'll excuse me, I have a very important date." She walks through them and follows the hostess to her table in the corner. Aarik watches her take her seat and his heart breaks.

"What are you thinking?" Ella asks.

"I just...I feel bad for her, you know?"

"No. Not really," Ella says. "If she wanted to be with people, she could. Maybe if she wasn't so coldhearted, she could make some friends."

"I know someone that seems just as coldhearted as the mistress right now." Aarik gives Ella a pointed look.

"No, that's not fair," Ella responds. "Elliot is just doing his job, he doesn't know he's being an ass."

"Not Elliot." Aarik waves her off. "You."

"Me? I have friends, and I'm on a date with a pretty boy. I'm not coldhearted."

"You're being coldhearted toward her." He points to the Mistress. "Wait, you think I'm pretty?"

"I wouldn't have put up with that silent date if you weren't something to look at."

Aarik gives a nod of appreciation, then turns to the Mistress. Without a second word he moves toward the woman sitting alone.

"Mistress Evergreen?" Aarik stands opposite the table of the Mistress. She looks up from her book. "I'm sorry for what I said earlier,"

"You mean thirty seconds ago?"

"Yes," Ella says, standing at Aarik's side.

Aarik looks between the women. "It's just, I'm so used to being surrounded by friends and family for the holiday that the idea of being alone is crazy to me."

"That must be nice; will that be all?" She looks back down at her book.

"Ok, good job." Ella tries to leave, but Aarik pulls her back.

"I mean to say, I don't think anyone should be alone on Semperlunas. And, well, it would mean a lot to me, and I'm sure it would mean a lot to the rest of the Penny Lich Guild, if you came to our party."

"You want me to come to your separatist's holiday party?" the Mistress asks.

"I mean, we can only afford it 'cause you keep giving us jobs. So, yeah, it'd be nice. Plus Hadvar and Gwen have been competing to make the best drinks, so you know there's gonna be some great booze."

"That's what we're hoping for at least," Ella says. At the mention of Hadvar and Gwen, the Mistress's eyes perk up. She then mulls over the suggestion like a fine wine, bites her lip, and looks around the Second Breakfast Cafe. After a moment, a couple passes her table and makes their way into the restroom. The lock shifts and the staff start getting a cleaning bucket ready.

Mistress Evergreen sighs and rolls her eyes. "Fine, I'll stop by when I get some work done."

"Great! I'm sure everyone will be thrilled," Aarik says. He looks over at Ella, who throws her hands in the air and lazily waves them about in celebration.

"Oh my Divine." This was about the tenth time Elliot had said that in the last minute.

"I know, right?" Sycilia says, nodding.

"Oh my freaking Divine." Elliot stares at a poster on the brickwall of a book and scroll store.

Semperlunas celebration with the Nooked Books, books and scrolls store. Come be a part of the festivities with spiced cider, cookies and a special guest. On tour for his newest book, The Latter Days of Small Town Heroes Reed Olenor will be joining us for a book signing and Q&A.

"Reed Olenor?" Elliot asks.

"Yeah, I saw all his books on your shelf,"

"Psh, not all his books," Elliot says, touching the painting of Reed on the poster. Elliot strokes his black hair, pointed goatee, and trim shirt. "I only have the Small Town Hero collection, or at least what's been released at this point. You see, they each follow a different character after the battle of the guardian from King City. You got Krontold, Dox, Mac, and Indriq. She's actually Reed's great great great aunt. So he has some special connections to the families. And of course, oh, of course there's Westra, my personal favorite."

"Oh?" Sycilia smiles at his exuberance.

"Well yeah, she's the one that struggles with two worlds, right? Her druidic nature and all, from her mother and the otherworldly magic that she gets from her father's bloodline. It's all very dramatic."

"You're crushing on a girl from two hundred years ago?"

"I mean, I wouldn't say I'm crushing on her. I think I just have a healthy respect for a woman that can overcome her situation to become one of the most powerful mages in Yonder Valley's history."

"Uh huh," Sycilia says. "Well, I got you the new book, and we're here for the meet and greet, so you better get all your questions about the mage hottie ready."

"Wait." Elliot spins so quickly his curls bob and his clothes flutter. "We're going in to meet him?"

"Yeah, that's why I brought you here"

"It wasn't for a job?"

"No. I lied. To get you here. Has no one ever surprised you before?"

"Just when Ella separated from me after using me to get close enough to a demon to kill it. That was pretty surprising."

"You getting divorced, or the demon part?

Elliot thinks for a second. Then tilts his head. "Getting dumped."

"Yeah, makes sense." Sycilia gets closer to Elliot, takes his hand, and begins leading him into the book store. Elliot blushes.

"Well enjoy this surprise," Sycilia says. "This is my gift to you."

Elliot and Sycilia sit in the audience watching the suave and sophisticated man speak. Sycilia looks at the attendees:clerics like Elliot, and young girls and boys and their parents. Oddly it's the parents who seem enraptured by the speaker and who seem to be holding books close to their chests.

Sycilia turns to see several wooden cut out figures painted and standing on either side of the author. One of the figures is a redheaded woman with wild and dreaded hair. She wears leafy green clothes and has tattoos on both arms. One arm is covered in inky black tentacles, and the other is green vines and vibrant flowers.

"Now it makes sense." Sycilia leans into Elliot, who is captivated by the man speaking.

"What?" Elliot dismissively whispers back.

"You have a thing for redheads." Sycilia smiles and points to Westra's cutout.

"What? No." Elliots blushes.

"You do. Look at you."

"That looks nothing like Ella."

"Other than the red hair, sure. Nothing. Though I do feel like I've seen her before."

"Probably on the book covers."

"Yeah, that must be it."

"Excuse me," Reed calls out to Sycilia, "did you have a question ma'am?"

"Me? No. Sorry, no." The crowd of teens, parents, and scribes look back at her, and she looks around as they begin to turn their attention back to the speaker. "But uh–" They all turn back to her. "This guy does." She points to Elliot. His face immediately runs red. Reed looks at the cleric and smiles.

"Well, I normally have questions wait until the proper time, but I think for the friend of such a beautiful figure such as yourself, I can make an exception."

"Oh, stop it," Sycilia says. "Come on, Elliot."

"Are you insane? I don't know what to say."

"Just tell him how important his books are to you," Sycilia whispers back.

"That's not a question."

"Then just pitch your voice up at the end, so it becomes one? Like that," Sycilia grabs a hold of Elliot and pulls him to his feet. A reminder of her strength.

"What's your name, sir?" Reed asks.

"Uh, I'm uh cleric." Elliot stumbles. "I mean I'm a cleric of Denier. Well, I was of Denier House, now I'm, I guess...freelance. I own the Penny Lich, and run a guild that helps people. And that's who I am, thank you, sir." Elliot tries to sit.

"That didn't answer my question, Cleric of the Penny Lich Guild," Reed says, smiling. The crowd laughs. Elliot laughs as well. He stands back up awkwardly.

"I'm uh, that is to say, my name is uh...well, it's uh, Elliot."

The crowd shifts its attention back to Reed.

"It's good to meet you, Mr. Elliot. What is your question?"

"Oh, uh, well, again, I run the Penny Lich and I was just the biggest fan of yours,"

"Was?" Reed asks, "I hope I didn't do anything to ruin that."

"No!" Elliot shouts. "No, I mean, er, I meant that before I was at the Penny Lich, I was in the Candle Crypts and I, uh, just spent my days reading books. And your detailed dive of the Small Town Heroes was always my favorite deep dive. And now, when I finally got a chance to get out of the temple basement, when I got my opportunity at life as an adventurer, I uh...." He turns back and sees Sycilia watching him. Then back at Reed.

"I got that opportunity and I took it. You uh, you sir, made me braver than I ever thought I would be." He turns to Sycilia again. "It's because of who you are, and what you do, that I'm free to choose my own path and be the man I want to." He looks back up at the author. "It's just you being you that teaches me everyday how to help the people around me."

Elliot sneaks a glance back at Sycilia. The crowd waits in silence, and Reed smiles a large smile. His eyes flicker between Elliot and Sycilia, then he clears his throat.

"I'm sorry, Elliot, but I don't think you actually asked a question."

"Oh, oh, right. I'm so sorry," Elliot says. "Uh , I actually was wondering what happened to OBE, the thing that visited Westra in her dreams during the battle of Valley Gate. Was that a cover name for something else?"

"Haha, yeah that's a great question, Elliot," Reed says. Standing up, he takes back the audience's attention and begins talking about the state of being that a dream creature takes and how it relates to metaphors within the mind, causing it to be vastly different than the true nature of the thing entering the dream from outside. Elliot watches him, still standing, forgetting that he was not the only one watching. Sycilia pulls him down slowly and smiles as he stakes his seat.

Hadvar makes his way into the basement of the Penny Lich. He works for a minute at the torch sitting by the door in front of the stairwell. After lighting it, he looks back to make sure no one is watching, and he dives into the dark cellar. Passing by wine racks, barrels of ale, whiskey, food, and peanuts, he makes his way to the back corner of the cellar where a wardrobe waits.

It is crafted to look old, which it achieves by being quite old. Ancient in fact. It stands eight feet tall and looks almost decrepit. The hinges are popped and cause the doors to hang slightly off the center. The knobs are faded, worn metal. The framing and molding are cracked and a musty smell of decay surrounds it. This is Hadvar's greatest treasure.

He presses his hands to the doors and strokes the splintering wood. "Home again, home again, jiggity jig."

He opens the six foot door and enters the wardrobe, empty of all things with easy access to the backboard. On the board are several markings that Hadvar quickly draws around with a piece of charcoal. After a moment sketching runes, he speaks soft words and the charcoal lines dig into the wood.

Hadvar steps out of the wardrop, closes the door and speaks his favorite word in the world. Suddenly the sounds of shifting, clanking, and wood tumbling down stairs rumbles from behind the wardrobe doors. He opens them and a warm bright light casts over him. The older gentleman smiles as he walks into the wardrobe, closing the doors behind him.

The inside of Hadvars multidimensional home is quaint and simple. Several large stone statues of bladed and armored men watch as he moves about the room, their eyes scanning him to be sure he is indeed the one who owns the place.

"Pete, Sue, Ed, Luce, hello," Hadvar says as he addresses each of them. "I know it's been some time. Is Alexander here still?" Hadvar looks out from the golems in waiting, through a set of arched glass windows. A great cavernous room is beyond the window. A golden light radiates from above, on a ceiling made of stone. Paintings of grandeur and beauty are carved, etched, and stained in reds and golds across this massive room. The light coming from a golden painting of the sun ripples with heat and moves across the mason sky, as a trail of distinct and separately colored moons trail behind it.

The room, which is as large as several city blocks, is littered with towering piles of books, treasures, and gems. Spiraling pillars of staircases reach from the floor to the ceiling throughout the great library, each stacked with books and trinkets from the worlds beyond.

A pile of books moves, and the ever slight ghostly figure streams toward him. It floats upward to where the balcony resides.

"How long has it been, sir?" the invisible being asks.

"Too long for sure, Alexander, but I'm afraid I can't stay for too long."

"A pity," the specter says. "I have read everything in here twice and have not had a single person to speak to about it. Your golems are very dull indeed, sir."

"They were made to protect, not entertain."

"I suppose." The specter sighs. "What can I retrieve for you?"

"I believe we have a recipe book of Hebenector, do we not?"

"Of course we do. What kind of multidimensional library would we be if we didn't keep the Cupbearer-to-the-god's recipes around. The real question is, why must I look for it?"

"I know this is going to sound petty, but the fact is, I've never faced such a foe in my life, and I need to come out as the victor of the encounter. So if I must tap into my magic reserves, then so be it."

"Would you like me to get your Grimander Inc., recall stone, just in case you need to make a quick escape?"

"No, no, there's no way this won't work. I have to beat my daughter at the cocktail contest. Or else what kind of dad would I be?"

"You guys made it just in time!" Gwen says as Elliot and Sycilia enter the Penny Lich. The sun is now past the zenith, and everyone is working on the last minute decorations for the Semperlunas night party.

"Syl, that was the most amazing. I mean, I still can't believe I spoke to him, and he spoke to me, and we spoke to each other. I mean, flip flappin' frack jacks, Syl, he knows my name."

"You meet another deity?" Moses asks hanging evergreen balls throughout the room. "You remember what happened last time you did that, right?" Potsticker, on cue, jumps into Elliot's arms.

Elliot pets the ball of fire, who closes its eyes and rubs into Elliot's chest.

"No, no, even better," Elliot says. Sycilia stands at the door watching, as Elliot walks over to Moses. "I met Reed Olenor. I met him, and he spoke to me, and he said my name."

"Who?" Moses asks. Elliot points to the book in Sycilia's hands. He begins explaining the characters and their story arcs and why they are each the best character in the series.

"–and it's all based on real events. All at the beginning of the Virgil Empire occupation of Yonder Valley–" Elliot continues to rant at Moses, who immediately regrets asking his single syllable question.

"He seems happy with his gift," Aarik says walking up to Sycilia, handing her a drink.

"Hey, I thought you were going on a date with Ella." Sycilia takes the drink.

"Eh, it was awkward. And when I asked her what she would like to do, she said 'drink somewhere familiar.'"

"Sounds exactly like her."

"Yeah, she's great." Aarik turns to the redheaded monster hunter at the bar. Ella watches Gwen get the drinks ready. He smiles and waves at her, while she awkwardly waves back with an uncomfortable smile. "But, uh, Elliot, he's really excited."

"It was really funny seeing him get all flustered and nervous,"

"You mean like he does all the time?"

Sycilia breathes out heavily. "Yeah, it's cute." Aarik's smirk turns to a grin, and he puts his hand on her shoulder.

"Ok, Dad!" Gwen calls out to the kitchen. "It's time!"

"One second!" Hadvar calls out from the kitchen.

"And Elliot and Sycilia are here, too, so you have to make the drink six times now."

"What?!" The voice booms from behind the door.

Hadvar sticks his head out and counts. “Fine, fine. One minute.” He hurries into the back of the kitchen, behind the pots and pans, in the pantry. In a small cauldron, a boiling liquid shimmers in gold and blue swirl. Green bubbles pop on its surface and release a misty foam.

Hadvar grabs six pint glasses and pours the concoction. The gold shimmer falls to the bottom of the glass, then the blue shifts to green. The liquid acts more like a heavy gas, and the pouring is like watching a fog roll in.

“This?” Hadvar says. “Just an old recipe I picked up from the Penny Lich in Haberdashery Woods. Magic? No, no, it’s...uh....” He practices his speech as he pours each glass. “Magic? No, no, just some fun dyes and tricks of light. Yes, well I am a very good bartender. No, no, you don’t have to worry, it’s not made with the ectoplasm of a twice dead spector from the ethereal realm. Or the gold used in a realm shift ritual. And it definitely does not have any stardust from the Krooom Desert Caverns. Haha. That would be insane. That would be something some half crazed wizard would feed his friends.” He stops and thinks for a moment as he’s about to finish the last pour. “That’s something a crazy person would give people.” His stare intensifies. “To feed them an Ethereal Ale without them knowing, that would...be something...a lunatic would do.” A moment of reflection passes.

Then, finishing the last glass, he finishes, “But a lunatic that has proven he is the greatest cocktail maker Valeward has ever seen. Never to be challenged by his daughter again!” He stands up straight with a tray of shimmering, misting, and gold swirling pint glasses. He walks out of the kitchen and into the tavern where his victims, uh, er...judges wait.

"This is an Ethereal Ale," Hadvar says as he hands his drink out. "So named for the uh, trick of the light from the ingredients used to create the swirling effect."

"Looks great!" Moses says downing the drink immediately.

"No, wait, I'm not done," Hadvar begins, but everyone takes their drinks and downs them. An all to common practice for the regulars at the tavern. They throw their heads back and Hadvar watches the the drinks disappear, "You're drinking them too fast! These are meant to be enjoyed over a long period of time."

And by the time he finishes saying that, the guild has emptied their glasses. Hadvar watches them for a moment. He hadn't tried it before he served it; he didn't know if he had gotten the concoction right. If he had put too much of anything in, it could be disastrous. They could be teleported to the Ethereal Realm in the blink of an eye. They could begin phasing out of solid matter and slide through the floor. They could pop. POP! What had he done!? He had let his obsession get the better of him. This is why he walked away from magic, why he stopped. It had gotten too real; it had too many consequences. It had changed the fate of his entire life and that of his daughter–that of the kingdom. No one knew, but he was responsible for it all! And he was hiding in plain sight, a criminal of absolutely unquenchable power. He had unleashed himself on the best people he had met in decades, and now they would begin to slide out of existan–

"This is really good, Hadvar," Brohn says.

"Seriously," Moses adds. "This is probably–oh my goodness–this is probably the best drink I've ever had. Even compared to the last one Gwen made."

"Really?" Hadvar lets loose a breath of relief. If he had done it right, the drink pulls from the Ethereal Realm and creates a taste on the tongue that comes from the drinker's imagination. It becomes the most delicious drink that they could ever possibly experience because it changes to be what they most desire. Hadvar stands and watches as the group describes the drink.

"It's like a sunset on the ocean, with bits of cherry wrapped up into a breakfast burrito," Aarik says.

Sycilia replies, "It's like an iceberg melting down, but it's made of candy and freshly baked bread."

"Oh, oh." Elliot points. "Like the winning point at a Scatterbattle match, and as a reward for being the greatest player in the world, you're dunked into a pool of melted cotton."

"That's what you taste?" Moses asks Elliot.

"Yeah, I mean, something like that."

"You're weird, man."

"So you guys like it?" Hadvar asks. "You don't feel off at all?"

"Off?" Ella asks.

"I feel a good buzz coming on," Aarik says.

"Well, ok, then. I think the judges have spoken," Hadvar says, turning to Gwen. "It's great that you want to be as good as me, honey boo, but I think it's clear that you're old dad is still champ."

"Hmm." Gwen walks past her dad and puts her shot glasses in front of the judges. A urine yellow colored liquid rests in each glass, and the judges all grimace as they inspect it.

"This is a Lemon Smucker Sucker Pop," Gwen says. She turns and watches her dad's face as the judges begin drinking the cocktail. The smug look on Hadvar's face drops and clings to Gwen's single raised eyebrow.

They all shoot and come up from the drink with bliss rolling over their faces.

"This is it," Aarik says. "This is the winner. Hands down, one hundred percent."

"One hundred and fifty thousand percent," Moses says.

"That's not a percentage," Elliot says. "But yeah, one hundred and fifty thousand percent that's the winner."

"It's so simple," Brohn says, tears growing in his eyes. He stares at the empty glass. "So simple, so powerful. It's so sad. It's gone, forever gone. It lives inside me now. Now I am the vessel for the divine." Brohn stands up. "I am the deity of the Lemon Smucker Sucker Pop! All hail me!"

Ella speaks up, "I'm speechless. I'm usually so eloquent, but now I am at a complete loss for words."

Sycilia chuckles a little. "You're all drunk. Hic. Drunk. Hic. You're shrunk." She laughs and covers her mouth.

Gwen watches the horror cross over her father's face as they clearly enjoy her drink more. She smiles and leans in to kiss him on the cheek. "Don't worry dad. Someday I'll teach you all I know about making drinks."

As the guild comes to their senses and finishes setting up for the party, the moons begin to peek out from behind the snow filled clouds. The Conclave begins its journey through the night sky giving light to the softly falling flakes. One descends over the city of clay roofs, and smoking chimneys down to the street where a group of young people make their way into the tavern. The wind catches the snowflake, sweeping it into the tavern, landing on a coat being taken off by an all too eager bard.

Barley in the door he sings a song that catches like fire and warms the room as others sing along. The bard begins playing his lute and brushes past a couple caught in a passionate kiss. The bard then jumps on a table where several men are eating a large meal, and he continues to play his song.

People from all over the city come into the Penny Lich to get a warm drink for comfort, and maybe a warm body for company, during the Semperlunas party. They sing songs that call out to the deities that watch down on them. The moons of Onto loom in the sky, like the watchful eyes of the Conclave. Snow peppers the streets and windows, the cold air pushing the party goers that much faster to the candle lit building in the city of Valward.

"Aren't you guys gonna join the festivities?" Brohn asks Aarik and Ella as they sit in the corner booth watching the tavern fill. Brohn moves about with Gwen, singing and swaying with several drinks in hand. The music turns to happier tunes, giving praise to those who lived through the year, singing of better off places beyond the vale of death–the warm hills of Evergreen, the hunting grounds of Thermala, the great drinking halls of ?, and lakes of endless fish in ?.

"We're still technically on our date," Aariks says.

"Then a drink for you both!" Brohn says. "For the best night of the year. And for a new romance kindled."

"You're a nut." Aarik laughs.

"He's quite right though," Ella says, taking the drink. "It is the best night of the year."

"Oh?" Aarik asks.

"The many moons have a certain paralyzing effect on dark creatures. It seemingly halts most monsters for a night. Perhaps it has to do with them hoping to be visited by their own loved ones passed."

"You really think the spirit of a dead person comes back to visit their family on Semperlunas night?" Aarik takes a drink.

"I do."

"Why?"

"I've seen it."

"Of course you have." Aarik laughs. "Was it a vampire lord you killed? Or let me guess, a ghoul you had slain, and it came back to visit its family, and you then slayed the entire village?"

"No,"

"Then what was it?"

"It was my father." Ella takes a swig.

"Your...your dad? He visited you?"

"Yes."

An awkward moment passes as Aarik waits for more. Ella continues to look at her drink.

"Well, what happened? You can't just leave it there," Aarik pushes.

"That's pretty much it," Ella responds. "He died in the pursuit of evil. I had no idea he died until he came to visit me on Semperlunas. Then he told me what I needed to know to get the men that got him."

"Oh my goodness. Oh my divine. Honey, that is so sad," Aarik says, scooting over to her side of the booth.

"Not really. I mean, I can see how it might seem that way, but I've said it before: it comes with the territory. The saddest that I've heard of is way worse than that. And it happened to–" She trails off.

"What?" Aarik asks, intrigued.

"I shouldn't say. It's personal and I don't want to lore dump again."

"First of all, I love all the lore in the world, feel free to go off. Second, if you have some juicy deets on someone I know, then I gotta know. You know?"

"You know the carol, 'The Child's Visit'?"

"The song Gwen sang this morning? Yeah."

"It was written about someone we know." Ella says, looking up at Aarik.

"Oh, you have to tell me. Please, Ella, please, oh Conclave, you gotta tell me."

"No, it's not right."

"Please, it can be my Semperlunas gift. I won't ask for anything else tonight. Unless you want me to ask for more tonight."

"Well, that doesn't seem fair," Ella says.

"What?"

Ella opens her hands. "I don't see my Semperlunas gift. I'm supposed to give you something, and you haven't gotten me anything?"

"Who said I haven't got anything for you?" Aarik smiles. He puts his fingers on Ella's face. Then strokes her hair gently and leans in.

"Aarik," Ella whispers. He holds back, inches from her lips. She can smell his breath, his hair, his neck. She can feel his skin. She breathes in deep and closes her eyes.

Aarik gently pulls her head forward and catches her with his lips. His tender touch radiates through her body, Aarik pushes his mouth between her lips and she can feel his hot breath as a smack of passion erupts between them. The caress lingers as they slowly pull away from their endearment.

"Aarik, I...whoa." Ella opens her eyes and sees Aarik's eyes beaming at her. His seductive mouth cracking into a smile of satisfaction.

"Now," he says in a low whisper, "all I want from you is to know who's got that sad story, little bee?"

Hadvar talks with several patrons as the door to the tavern opens with a swarm of newcomers. Gwen is quick to help them off load their coats. One of them sneaks past the others and makes her way into the room. The warm light reflects off her skin and graying hair. Her jacket covers her entire torso and arms, gloves covering hands.

"Mistress Evergreen?" Hadvar says as she makes her way to the bar. He freezes.

"Hadvar," the Mistress says in greeting. " I was told that this is where I might be able to find some of Valewards best libations this evening."

"You're in my bar," the older gentleman says. "On Semperlunas. Are you dead? Did you die?"

"Please." The Mistress dismisses his accusation. "As if I would come back to visit you before passing on."

"Then, why are you here?" Hadvar says, still frozen.

"Aarik invited her," Gwen says as she comes around the woman. "Hi, I'm Gwen." She sticks out her hand to the older woman and beams a great smile. The Mistress stares at Gwen for a moment, unmoving, absorbing the sight of her. A small slip of a smile forms on the woman's face, but soon moves on.

"I'm Hadvar's–"

"Child?" The Mistress asks.

"Daughter," Gwen corrects.

"Interesting. Hadvar you never said you had a... daughter."

"You know my dad?"

"I do."

"She doesn't," Hadvar corrects. "I mean to say, er, she knew me from back in the day, when we were young, but she doesn't know me now. In my old age." He glares at the Mistress. "A lot has changed."

"Can I take your coat? You must be sweltering in

that thing," Gwen offers.

"I'm fine, thank you."

"Are you sure?" Gwen says, gesturing.

"I'm quite sure, thank you. I don't think I'll be staying long. I just came for a drink, and then I think I have a meeting I must attend."

Gwen walks over to Hadvar's side of the bar. Hadvar is still uncomfortable, his face is stoic.

"You have to work tonight?" Gwen says preparing several drinks from below.

"Oh, you know how those corporate folks are–ever Grim, ever watching," the Mistress says, watching Hadvar.

"Well, here you go. This is one of my Lemon Smucker Smacker Pops. This will help you relax a little, guaranteed." She slides forward the drink. The Mistress regards it, then picks it up and sniffs it.

"I do say, this is quite the little concoction you have here." She raises it to her lips. "A lemon...Suck Smack?"

"Lemon Smucker Smacker Pop."

'Right. Of course." Condescension drips from her smackers. She throws the drink back. In the time it takes for her head to go back upright, she has changed, and slams the glass on the bar. She looks at Gwen with a deadly serious look. Her eyes shift from the girl to her father, then back to the girl.

"Another," the Mistress says.

"Oh, I think the limit is one per customer," Hadvar says.

The Mistress breathes in slowly with her eyes closed. She speaks slowly and directly. "Give me another."

"Yes ma'am," Hadvar says. Without taking his eyes off the woman, he speaks to Gwen. "Come on Yoboh, give the woman another smacker."

"Lemon Smucker Smack–"

"Just do it," Hadvar shouts, causing Gwen to fumble.

"Here–Here you go." Gwen slides a second shot to the mistress. The woman immediately lifts the drink to her lips, thinks for a moment, then downs it. She comes off the drink slower than the last one, savoring the flavor.

"You made this drink?" the Mistress asks Gwen. Gwen nod's nervously. "Let's talk over a couple more."

"Me?" Gwen asks.

'Yup, yup, let's go." The Mistress walks to an empty table. "Don't forget more of those." Gwen turns to her dad, who cringes with an inability to help her. He reaches down and grabs a tray of Lemon Smucker Smacker Pops and gives it to his daughter.

"Come on girly!" the Mistress says from the table.

"Good luck," Hadvar says.

"Sycilia!" Elliot shouts over the crowd. Sycilia is speaking to several people by the fire about a recent quest. Elliot throws his hand in the air and waves at the girl. She looks up and smiles at him, dismissing the two men near her.

"Hey," Elliot says nervously.

"Hey," Sycilia says, tucking several dreads behind her ears.

"So uh, I just wanted to say thank you for earlier today, you know," Elliot says.

"You already thanked me Elliot, like twenty times." Sycilia chuckles. "I mean, don't get me wrong, what I did was great and deserving of like, a hundred thank yous, but you know...."

"Of course, of course," Elliot says. He then bows. "Then I shall continue to thank thee until I have met the quota." He pretends to tip his hat. "Thank you, my lady. Thank you for such a wonderful gift."

"Oh." Sycilia fans her face, playing along. "I do declare that is quite generous of you."

Elliot bows down on one knee. "Of course, all the thanks be to you, my queen of Semperlunas. I shall say it again and again–Thank you, thank you, a thousand times thank you.'"

"You're just too much, my good sir. Please go on," Sycilia throws her hands on her forehead.

They chuckle. Then realize that Moses and Gwen are watching them.

"Did you guys see that?" Elliot asks, standing up.

"Yup," Moses says.

'Like, right at the end there or–"

"All of it," Gwen says. "We saw everything."

"That was the cringiest thing I've ever seen," Moses says.

Elliot stands up quickly. "Well, it's from earlier. 'Cause of her gift."

"No, I get it. But...don't." Moses gags. "Sorry, I was just playing back in my head–" He gags again. "Oh, Divine, no."

"Hey!" Sycilia starts moving toward Moses, but Gwen puts her hand up.

"Before you beat him to death," Gwen says, "you have to dance during the Concha Walz. And you have to dance with Elliot."

"What?" Both Sycilia and Elliot protest. "Why?"

"No!" Elliot says. Sycilia looks at him with anger. "I mean, not that I don't want to dance with you, I mean I would love to. Not love, I mean, I will dance with you if I'm forced to, or rather, not forced, forced is a bad word. I will dance with you because It is... Cause I will dance with you."

"You're gosh dern right you'll dance with me," Sycilia says. She then turns to Gwen. "But why are you doing this?"

"You two are under the Mask of Aster." She points to the mask staring down at Elliot. He shutters. "Everyone else is free to choose a partner, but tradition says two people found in the sight of Aster at the end of twilight must dance together to appease the Conclave. It's the rules." Gwen spins her fingers and the bard and band begins to play a song for couples.

Gwen and Moses walk away from Elliot and Sycilia. "That wasn't Aster, that was just some rando mask of a nobody saint," Moses says as they move into the crowd.

"Yeah, but they don't know that," Gwen says. Moses smiles as he realizes what Gwen is doing, he puts his hand out, Gwen slaps it and they laugh with machiavellian glee.

The music begins to swell as the bard lets loose his song of love. It is a hymn of rejoicing in a year passing by as two lovers find each other in the dark night of Semperlunas. A celebration of gentle caresses and kisses. A swooning and swaying song of surviving the harsh world, only to be side by side with the one who will hold them in the cold, dark night.

Elliot laughs nervously, as Sycilia walks toward the dance floor. Elliot adjusts his glasses and moves with her. Sycilia laughs, realizing she was too ready to make a move.

"I uh, guess, we should...." Elliot says, leading his hand out to help her find her way.

'Yes, well, tradition and all," Sycilia says.

"Damn the gods and their ways," Elliot says in mock anger.

"Yes, well...." Sycilia throws her hands out a bit.

"Oh, right, yes, shall we dance?" Elliot asks.

"Yes, of course."

Elliot puts his hands out and waits for Sycilia to take hold. She smiles while reaching out. Then flinches slightly and chuckles nervously before she takes hold. Her hands are gentle in Elliot's grasp, and he wraps his arm around her waist and holds her close. A flutter of nervous energy passes between them. He leads while holding her, rubbing the back of her hand with his thumb. Glistening sweat on her dark skin reflects the light of the tavern into his starry eyes.

"I haven't danced in years," Sycilia says.

"I've not danced since my wedding," Elliot says. "And I immediately regret saying that."

"No, it's fine," Sycilia says, letting go of his shoulder to lift his head up. "I understand." Her smile challenges him, the nervous energy passes, and they begin moving as one. Sycilia lets Elliot take the lead. The song is beautiful, the music waltzing back and forth, pushing couples closer and closer as they step in time to the string's harmony.

After a moment, Sycilia wraps her arms around Elliot's neck and leans in. Her head resting on his shoulder, she listens to his breath. Nervous and catching, his heart beats quickly. She smiles and breathes in his scent. For a moment she forgets about the world, about her past, about everything. She lets him hold her, both hands around the waist. This is a hug--an embrace. She has never felt this. She's never been in–

"Syl," Elliot says, slowing. She opens her eyes and pops her head up, "The, uh, the song is over. I think we're in the clear."

Sycilia looks around and sees that the band is beginning a new song–faster and more group oriented. "Right. Well, whew. Glad that's over, eh?" She leaves his clasp, trying to get away quickly, but he catches her hand.

"Actually," Elliot says, as she turns back around. "I was hoping to give you this." She looks down and in his other hand is a box. Small, made of wood, and with a pink ribbon wrapped in a bow around the top.

"What is it?" Sycilia asks, touching the bow.

"It's a gift for Semperlunas."

"You got me a gift?" Her voice sings of genuine excitement and confusion.

"Well, I had to do something. I knew you were gonna take me to the book signing."

"You knew?" Her shock pulls her away from the box being handed to her.

"Your brother is the biggest gossip I've ever met, but hey, before you go throttle him, hold on." Elliot laughs as he holds her back. "Open this."

She turns back around and takes a hold of the tiny chest. The ribbon comes off easy enough, and her eyes gleam in excitement as she opens it.

"I know, this might seem weird for a couple reasons," Elloit says. Syscila pulls the wooden ring out of the box and holds it up in the light. "Why give you a onering?"

"This is a onering?" she hisses at him. "What are you doing with a onering?"

"No, no, wait." Elliot throws his hands up. "It's spent, it was used. It's safe. And the Mistress knows I have it. And yeah, I get it, it's weird cause why give you a used onering? But look, this is the ring you used to help me win this place. This is the ring of invisibility."

"Really?" She looks at it with a new interest.

"Yeah, and I actually had a new inscription done inside," Elliot points to the inside of the ring.

"In a moment when you need it most, be brave," Sycilia reads.

"Sycilia," Elliot starts, "if it hadn't been for you, this place wouldn't exist. I mean, it would, it would just be different. But I wouldn't exist, you know? Because of you I found a new place in this world, I push myself, and I'm free. You and this dumb little ring are responsible for everything good in my life now. I just wanted some way to remind you of that. That everyday you're alive is a day that this world is better for it. I just wanted to say, well...I guess I just wanted to say thank you."

As she receives her gift, Sycilia sniffles.

"Oh my Divine, I'm sorry, it's a shitty gi--" Elliot starts, but before he can get any further Sycilia reaches out and grabs him. She throws her arms around him and hugs him tight. His glasses go askew and he feels his bones compress. The larger woman holds him as close as possible, keeping him from leaving.

"Thank you, Elliot," she whispers.

Hadvar watches as Gwen moves about the room. She serves her drinks, encouraging people to dance. She sings and drinks with her friends. The drink in Hadvar's hand swirls, the gold and blue meshing in a hazy pattern. The joy of the night is muffled by Hadvars concerns, the drink in his hand almost untouched.

"Hey, man!" Moses says as he hands the older gentleman a bit of food. Hadvar continues to watch his daughter. "You doing ok? You've seemed off all night? Is it 'cause the Mistress is here?"

"What? No," Hadvar says dismissively. "I mean, yeah she kinda brings down the whole party." They both look down the bar and see the prim and proper Mistress sitting alone, watching the crowd.

"She needs to get laid," Moses says. He swings his head around and looks at Hadvar. Hadvar chuckles.

"There's no way that's gonna happen," Hadvar says, bringing the drink up to his lips, then quickly says, "Not again."

Moses' mouth drops and he stifles a howl of approval. "Hadvar, you dog." Hadvar sips his drink, blushing slightly. Afterward, he hisses in satisfaction, and shakes his head.

"You know that drink you made was absolutely fantastic," Moses continues. "And you should be proud of Gwen for being able to make a drink better than that."

"That's the thing, Moses," Hadvar says. "There's no possible way her drink was better than mine."

"How can you say that? She's a great bartender. Maybe she just has a gift, man."

"I don't doubt it. But, Moses, you're the only person here that knows parts of my past. You know what I'm capable of."

"Yeah, so? You said you don't use magic anymore. Said you gave it up to cultivate a better life for yourself so you can take care of Gwen bett– Oh my Deities, that drink was magic." Moses points at the glass Hadvar holds up as evidence. "You made me drink magic? Am I going to turn into a toad?"

"No, if that was gonna happen it would have already."

"What?" Moses looks horrified. "You're saying there was a chance?"

"Shh, look man," Hadvar whispers. "I made a drink with magic that was impossible to beat. And yet Gwen did."

"She's built different, what can I say?"

"No, Moses, you're not getting it," Hadvar says. "The only possible way to beat my drink–" He holds up his glass of swirling mist, "--is to use magic."

Moses thinks for a moment. An idea of what Hadvar is getting at begins to sink in. "Oh my word, you think...."

"Yeah...."

"You think someone switched out Gwens drink for a magic potion."

"What?" Hadvar pulls back, "No. Moses, she's a witch."

"What?" Moses looks over at Gwen, "Nooooo. What? But she's so innocent, and pretty, and good looking, and nice, and cute, and attractive and–"

"Hey, she's still my daughter."

"Right."

"Well." Hadvar takes the final swig of his drink. "Looks like I'll have to do something I've been dreading doing for my entire parenting career."

'What's that?"

Hadvar looks at the Mistress and clicks his tongue. "Tell my daughter the truth."

After getting a degree in film and media, T.W. Clawson realized that he didn't want to make movies, he wanted to get married, and write stories. It was while he was unemployed and homeless that he started to accomplish both of those dreams. He began writing badly written novels and since then learned how incredibly terrible he is at it.

Thankfully he persisted and uses his podcast, Between Lewis & Lovecraft as well as his serial shorts as a way to grow. All the while learning to be a better man for his wife and newborn son. He pretends to live in the Pacific Northwest but really lives between pages of his favorite books.

You can follow his adventures and get updates on The Penny Lich by signing up for his newsletter through his website;

TWClawson.com

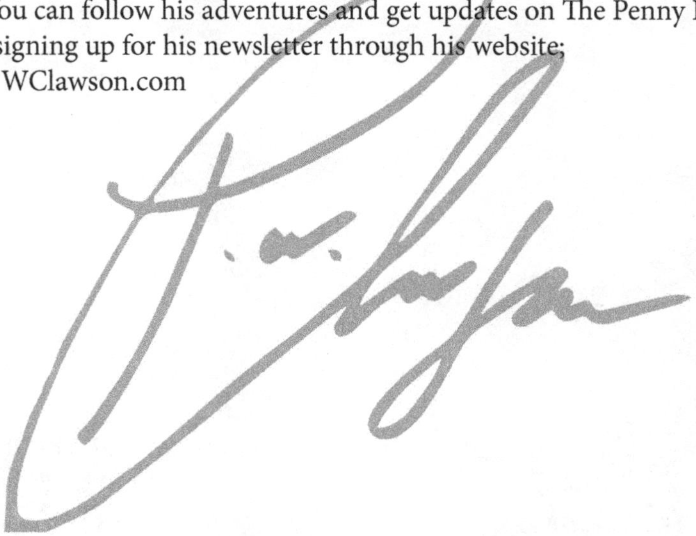

CPSIA information can be obtained
at www.ICGtesting.com
Printed in the USA
JSHW020729140723
44724JS00003B/29

9 781736 461860